The Magic Lantern

From Ross- Bremner
Tain
Christmas 2014.

ALSO BY HAMISH ROSS

NON-FICTION

Paddy Mayne

Freedom in the Air

From SAS to Blood Diamond Wars

FICTION

Wrongs Hushed Up

The Magic Lantern

Two Novellas

HAMISH ROSS

Duthac Books

First published in 2014 by

Duthac Books
6 Skaterigg Gardens
Glasgow
G13 1ST
Copyright © Hamish Ross 2014

Hamish Ross has asserted his right under the Copyright,
Designs and Patents Act 1988 to be identified as the
author of this work.

Lines from Edwin Morgan's 'The Death of Marilyn
Monroe' published by Edinburgh University Press in
Scottish Poetry – Number One, eds. George Bruce,
Maurice Lindsay and Edwin Morgan are quoted by
permission of the publisher.

ISBN 978-0-9570888-2-5

Printed and bound in recycled paper by

Clydeside Press Ltd
37 High Street
Glasgow
G1 1LX

For Elisabeth

La photographie, c'est la vérité, et le cinema, c'est vingt-quatre fois la vérité par seconde.

(Photography is truth, and cinema is truth 24 times per second.)

from the film *Le Petit Soldat,* written and directed by Jean-Luc Godard

CONTENTS

The Magic Lantern

In the wake of the slaughter in the trenches, Remembrance Day in the small Highland town that sacrificed a hundred and twenty-two men to the god of war held a powerful emotive charge.

The Rev John Cameron, with Military Cross and campaign medals on his cassock, glanced down at the index card he used as a prompt for his sermon. In his neat handwriting: 9 November 1930, Psalm 6, v. 5; Film, *All Quiet on the Western Front.*

The church was filled to capacity; the centre part was occupied by a detachment of the Territorial Army, the British Legion war veterans and the uniformed youth organisations, the Boy Scouts and the Girl Guides. At the start of the service he had stood at the front and beckoned the congregation to rise; and two standard bearers, carrying the Union Jack and the British Legion colours, slow-stepped to the front to have the flags received. The National Anthem was sung; and the order of service commenced.

John Cameron looked up from the index card.

'"For in death there is no remembrance of thee: in the grave who will give thee thanks?" the psalmist writes.'

Looking round the packed congregation, he said slowly, 'Life was very dear to those men we remember here today. When the demonic power of

1

weaponry threatened annihilation; even when . . .' there was a catch in his voice, 'even when it seemed that God had abandoned them, they never lost their love of life and beauty in life.

'I can think of no better way to illustrate how strong those feelings were than to speak about the final scenes of the film that was shown at the cinema last week: *All Quiet on the Western Front.*

'It's an American film, but from the German viewpoint,' the minister continued.

John Cameron, both hands on the lectern, looked directly at areas of the congregation, 'Yes. The enemy soldiers, whose concerns and priorities, as any veteran sitting here will tell you, were exactly the same as ours.'

Willie Meikle, a solemn figure in his black three-piece Sunday suit, lifted his eyes from the open hymn book on the pew. When the minister brought the word film into the sermon, a scowl fell upon his brows. As the minister continued, it darkened.

'In the film's closing scenes,' the minister went on, 'a young soldier, the only survivor of the original group he'd enlisted with, stretches out his hand through the rifle embrasure in the trench to attract on to his finger a butterfly that appears during a period of quiet, when the guns are silent. The butterfly, this delicate, beautiful creature fluttering into the battlefield just within a foot or two of the trench.' John Cameron gestured with outstretched arm beyond the pulpit.

Helen Ross, in her early thirties, a guide leader, sitting in the centre area with the Girl Guides, had lost her fiancé, killed in action in 1916. She clenched her fists and dug her fingernails into her palms. The minister's words burned an image in her mind of their last walk that lovely spring day; the skylark high above. She tried to stop her tears. She didn't want the girls to see her crying.

'The soldier reaches out,' the preacher went on. 'He wants it to alight on his finger for a moment. He can't quite reach; he raises his head and shoulders above the parapet and stretches further. He is seen from the enemy trenches. A sniper carefully adjusts his sights . . .'

In a side pew to the left, fifteen-year old Andrew Douglas sat with his mother. He'd seen the film on Friday evening. It had had a big effect on him; it gave him the insight he needed to make a decision about his future, a decision that he and his mother had argued over all Saturday evening. He felt reassured as he listened.

John Cameron paused, 'That picture of the young soldier reaching out for life and for beauty reaffirms, for me, what we yearn for and hold dear to; even when God seems very remote from us . . .'

Andrew's mother, a war widow, lowered her head. Although it pained her as she thought about it, she came to a decision during the service.

'. . . their language was not always of the best; many blasphemed. But I remember them for their love of life; and we, here today, give thanks for their finest qualities . . .'

Stuart Robertson, Manager of the Town Hall Cinema, a wartime pacifist, who had spent time in prison for refusing to be conscripted in 1916, sat in the gallery. An atheist, he hadn't been in a church for seventeen years. He listened attentively to a man he had come to respect.

Forty-eight hours earlier on Friday morning, shortly before 9am, Stuart Robertson opened the cinema's double doors from the inside, and stood a moment, holding each leaf wide apart the extent of his arms' reach, framed between the pillars supporting the central arch of the Romanesque frontage. He was in his middle thirties, of medium height and was slimly built; he had his hair cut short; he hadn't followed the long, slicked-back style of the latest Brylcreem advertisements.

It had been a frosty night, and the sky was bright and clear; the crisp November morning air flooded into the foyer, flushing out the familiar fug of last night. Across the way, on the other side of Tower Street, Duncan Christie had already opened his grocery shop, and was now wheeling out the delivery bike on to the pavement to prop it up on its stand. Stuart looked down the steep flight of steps of what had once been the Town Hall. Hoar-frost lay on the handrails wherever bare metal was exposed, as though some phantom confectioner had decorated the flaked paintwork with icing during the night. He walked each leaf of the door, in turn, through a hundred and eighty degree arc and secured it to its wall fixing.

On the wall beyond both doors were the glass-fronted display units for the stills. As he was removing the stills for W D Griffith's first talking picture, *Abraham Lincoln*, the clip-clop of hooves and the trundle of iron-clad wooden wheels on the roadway stopped outside the grocery. A drayman began unloading sacks of potatoes. Griffith's movie played on Wednesday and Thursday. Despite the present economic hardships, attendances at the cinema were holding up. Stuart was optimistic about full houses for the next film to be screened on Friday and Saturday, Lewis Milestone's *All Quiet on the Western Front.* While he waited for John Cameron, he went into the foyer and spread out the selection of stills on the desk. Although the distributors hadn't given the cinema manager much of a choice when it came to posters, there was a fair range of stills to choose from; he selected judiciously and was closing the display units, as John Cameron climbed the cinema steps.

Stuart greeted him warmly. An unlikely friendship had developed between the two men since they found themselves on a discussion panel, talking to senior pupils at the academy about career choice.

'It's very good of you to put on this showing for me. I can't manage the evening performances. I think I mentioned that I've meetings. But you're sure you're not wasting staff time?' John said.

'No, it's standard practice for us to run through the main feature in the morning of its showing in case there are breaks in the print.'

'Aren't you lucky to have it so soon; didn't it win a prestigious prize this year?'

'It won two Academy Awards this year: one for best film and the other for best director. So yes, we've been lucky. I requested it for the two days leading up to Remembrance Sunday. Didn't have high hopes though.'

But he had caught the attention of senior officials at head office. He had been an energetic and effective assistant manager in Glasgow; and it was thought that he had the experience and gravitas to represent the company in the small, main town of Easter Ross that was to have a cinema for the first time.

He and John Cameron walked a short way into the empty hall. The inner doors had been closed during the night and the high ceilinged old building held the trapped, acrid smell of stale cigarette smoke. Stuart turned round to George Anderson, the projectionist, who was looking through the projection window waiting for the signal to begin.

For all the years he'd worked in the business, Stuart still felt that thrill of anticipation at this moment, when the overhead lights dimmed and the shaft of bright light pierced the length of the auditorium and the silver screen came alive, as the magic lantern took you into another realm.

It never palled for him, the transformation of a disparate group of people sitting idly talking, facing the curtained proscenium arch: the screen appears; the credits come up; and an audience is created and transported to other worlds and cultures, reacting to the story, becoming part of the story, and responding to the film's editing, its rhythm and pace. Sometimes he would vary the moment by standing in the projection box as the reel of film unwound on the clicking sprockets and he would watch the screen through the second projection window. One person was in complete control. Unlike live theatre, here the actors were ghosts in the machine; you allowed them to appear and to disappear.

His fascination for the darkened room and the crystal-sharp image began when he was at school, in a small town not unlike this one. One day during the summer holidays, he and a pal found something to do helping an elderly gentleman, a former provost of the town, to polish his Argyll sedan car. Provost MacRae was portly, with a ruddy face, and he had difficulty bending to wipe the chamois over the hubcaps and wheel arches and even the running board.

After they had finished, Provost MacRae invited them to rummage in the loft space above the garage to see if they could find anything of interest to them. There they found an old magic lantern that hadn't been used for years. And there were boxes of glass slides. The old gentleman explained how it worked, and said they could keep it and the slides for the duration of the school summer holidays; and he arranged with its caretaker to give them a key to the Oddfellows' Hall. They gave shows to their families, but mainly it was for themselves that they projected images. And what inspired Stuart was that they could create stories; they did it through their choice of images and the order they placed them in. They used the entire set of slides, from shots of famous buildings of the world to characters from history.

A beam of light from the projection box lit up the screen. The first reel ran; the film's credits rolled; both men, cinema manager and the church minister, sat in the empty theatre. Then a stark prologue appeared on the screen and stayed on for longer than it took to scan the words.

'This story is neither an accusation nor a confession, and least of all an adventure, for death is not an adventure to those who stand face to face with it. It will try simply to tell of a generation of men who, even though they may have escaped its shells, were destroyed by the war.'

The words gave way to images of civilians and soldiers making ready for war.

Helen Ross walked along Tower Street to her office. Her dark curls bobbed beneath her cloche hat as she walked, and her calf-length, green plaid coat outlined her neat figure. She drew level with the memorial on the old Tolbooth wall and looked at it as she passed. Although she knew its words by heart, she felt it would be a betrayal not to acknowledge it. The memorial had been dedicated five years after the war ended. At first, its words reawakened her grief; then grief changed to anger; and finally anger became stoical acceptance. There would never be an end to it, to wars and killing. The memorial's overarching aggressive-looking design of an antlered stag's head and under it the Gaelic motto, *Cuidich 'n Righ* (help the king) and the defiant final words in larger lettering all spoke of a warlike spirit:

ERECTED BY
THE SEAFORTH HIGHLANDERS
TO THE UNDYING MEMORY OF 8432
COMRADES BELONGING TO THE TEN
BATTALIONS OF THE REGIMENT
WHO GAVE THEIR LIVES FOR THEIR

COUNTRY IN THE GREAT WAR
SCOTLAND FOR EVER

She was in good time for work, and, on the spur of the moment, she turned left a little way past the Tolbooth, walked down Castle Brae and went into the medieval Collegiate Church of St Duthac.

It was now a chilling empty shell of a building, bereft of church furniture, not at all welcoming. She felt it resented her intrusion and the sound of her heels on the flagstone floor echoing within its walls, as though it was still nursing a grievance at having been stripped of its former status. She walked along by the north wall to the bronze memorial plaque on which were etched the names of 122 townsmen who had fallen in the Great War. Stretching out her hand, she traced her ring finger over Alan's name. The barest information: rank, initial, surname and unit. But the symbols bore no relation to the man she loved. It was like her recurring dream where she was looking for Alan, but couldn't find him in masses of men in khaki.

She closed her eyes and focussed on memory. They were sweethearts at school. He was the year ahead of her. Then came August 1914, and Alan was caught up in the first wave of jingoism that laved through the country; he hadn't waited to finish school. He joined the Seaforth Highlanders.

When he came home on leave before going to France, he was more mature than the senior schoolboy who had left the town. And he was handsome in uniform, with the rakish tilt of the Balmoral bonnet and the pleats of the Mackenzie tartan kilt swinging in rhythm with his step.

9

The atmosphere had changed because of this war, and they were both caught up in it. It was as though currents of electricity flowed around them, and they were in the centre of a force field, and they acted as though there were roles they were constrained to play.

It had been that lovely day in early May 1915, and they walked the four miles to Culpleasant. Clumps of gorse in full bloom by the roadside were golden plumes, flagging their route. 'Remember when we skipped school that afternoon in late spring, when you were in fourth year?' Alan said.

She laughed, 'The fuss they made! You'd have thought we'd eloped.' She tightened her hold on his hand, looked into his eyes and said, 'Sing "Wild Mountain Thyme" like you did that day.'

> 'Oh the summer time is coming,
> And the trees are sweetly blooming,
> And the wild mountain thyme . . .'

He had a lovely folk-singing voice and swung effortlessly, without pause, into the song.

> 'Will ye go lassie go?
> And we'll all go together
> To pick wild mountain thyme . . .'

Walking hand in hand, swinging joined hands in time to the melody and their stride, they turned off the road and walked to Strathrory.

'Do you think couples came to places like this in earlier times?' she said.

'Yes, at mid-summer, or the spring equinox.'

The hills to the west were violet-blue. The air was perfectly still; not a breath of wind stirred; faintly, from far above came the song of the lark. Her nuptial bed was under the canopy of heaven, in a little grassy hollow dotted with primroses.

He was more confident, having lived among men. But he had not been coarsened; he was tender towards her and inexperienced.

As she stood by the memorial, the last verse Alan sang that day echoed for her,

> 'If my true love she were gone
> I will surely find no other
> Where wild mountain thyme...'

She could feel her eyelashes wet with tears.

After his embarkation leave, she got letters via the British Expeditionary Force, with amusing tales of the foibles of comrades; descriptions of fields of mud and horse-drawn vehicles, as though it was all some prairie-wide expedition; the enemy (hardly ever mentioned) was personified as Jerry; and always there was forced cheerfulness. It went on like that until late in 1916. First a whispered rumour reached the office; and they told her; in dread she ran to the newsagent for a paper with the recent casualty lists; scanning the names, eyes refusing to read the words, hoping desperately not to find his, until that moment of sheer anguish. The brutal information: serial number, name, unit.

Blinded by tears, refusing to accept...

When the final reckoning came, the cost to the small burgh was far in excess of anything they could have anticipated. Nothing had prepared them for the extent of the sacrifice. Lines from the old Scots ballad lamenting loss at the Battle of Flodden resonated for Helen and many women:

> Lassies a-lilting before dawn o' day;
> But now they are moaning, on ilka green loaning,
> The Flowers of the Forest are a' wede away.

Carried off by death too were her prospects, like those of so many women who had to fend for themselves, and accept their lot. So, gradually, her grief became subsumed into that of the many.

Helen considered herself to be a war widow. She learned fortitude, though, from her mother, who had lost her husband in an accident at work on the railways down south. And Helen made a life for herself. She thought if she was not to have the satisfaction of motherhood, of having her own family, she could help influence the lives of young girls. She became a guider, and the Girl Guide movement became her main interest outside work. Tonight the company were going to rehearse their part in the Remembrance Day parade with the other uniformed organisations.

She opened her eyes and faced the present. All that was left of a life, of love: symbols on a bronze plaque. She felt cheated. Death had claimed these men; they all merged in death, like in her recurring dream. And she felt that she was an intruder. Suddenly, she regretted the impulse that made her come into the Collegiate Church. She left, her steps echoing mockingly in the sepulchral silence.

She arrived at the office where she worked, the old established firm of Henry Sangster & Son, Solicitors and Notary Public. Those words had been etched on the inner glass-bevelled door more than fifty years ago. The firm was so old that the son, who had no issue, was now in his sixties. But in the spring of the year, David Sangster told her he was bringing in a younger partner, Archie MacNair, who was unmarried, in his early-forties and a veteran of the war.

Helen found that the new partner was impeccably courteous. He also liked being frank about himself. After he had had a meeting with an old client, whose legal affairs the firm had looked after for decades, she'd brought in a cup of coffee to Archie's office, and was waiting for a briefing on the outcome. But instead, Archie lapsed into reflective mood, while she listened. He mused on the futility of acquiring wealth and possessions, in order to pass them on to future generations. That was not for him. He told her he'd been wounded at the second battle of the Somme; his life, he'd been told, hung in the balance for days; he considered himself very lucky to have survived. He had no intention of surrendering to domesticity — he was going to cherry-pick his way along life's path. He had taken a room in one of the hotels in the town; and soon she heard that he'd acquired the reputation of being a womanizer. She could tell that he found her attractive, but he seemed to have assessed she was a woman who would be interested only in a stable relationship, not in dalliance.

After working to him for a few months, Helen began to suspect that he was not being honest about himself: the war had destroyed something in Archie. He'd been an officer, who had led men, but now, she felt, he was evading responsibility and commitment. She wondered if, by living only for the moment, he might become pathetic in time.

'Wool-gathering won't help you answer questions in an interpretation paper Andrew. It may give you ideas for an essay, but the solutions you're looking for here are in the text,' Miss Johnston said, standing in front of Andrew Douglas's desk, pointing to the practice test paper in front of him.

He reddened, and turned his attention to the practice paper for the Lower Level Certificate. He didn't want to come down in English or in any of his subjects. And he had to work all the harder at them because he had an evening and Saturday job as a delivery boy at Christie's Grocery. But what happened yesterday evening had completely thrown him; the events, sometimes in sequence, sometimes out of sequence, went round in his head in a continual loop.

Duncan Christie had closed the outer double doors to, but hadn't yet slipped the bolt across from the inside — as though he was expecting someone to come by. He went behind the counter, reached up and took down a glass jar with coffee beans. He unscrewed the top, gripped the jar by the rim with his right hand and, pressing it with his arm against his side, tilted it and spilled some beans into his cupped left hand. Then he leaned forward across the counter, and with a dextrous flick of his left wrist, sent them scattering across the floor. Andrew knew the drill and trod on a few beans; the others would remain to be trodden in by customers tomorrow morning. And this simple trick brought about a transformation overnight in the closed shop: the crushed beans gave out the aroma of coffee that gradually permeated the store; and customers added to the process in the morning, so that an atmosphere redolent of fresh coffee filled the store overwhelming the multitudinous odours given off by green vegetables, fruit, the earthy open bag of potatoes and the large cheddar cheese that sat on the counter during the day.

A few minutes later, Stuart Robertson pushed against the closed door and came into the store. He was dressed as cinema manager in evening suit and black tie. He and Duncan nodded to each other, but he came over to Andrew, his black shoes crushing coffee beans as he came, 'How would you like to like to work in the cinema as a trainee projectionist?' He paused a moment to let the question fully register with Andrew, then smiled and followed up with, 'You would work under George, who's an experienced hand. And you're a keen film fan. You would like the work.'

It had come right out of the blue.

'I . . . I'm not sure,' was all he could stumble out. In a split second his thoughts went round the compass: he spun from bewilderment to elation to anxiety.

'That's all right. Take the week-end to think about it. Talk it over with your mother. Let me know what you've decided on Monday.'

After Stuart and Duncan Christie exchanged a few pleasantries, Stuart left the shop, giving Andrew a reassuring smile as he went.

'That's a good offer Stuart Robertson's making you,' Duncan said, as though reading Andrew's thoughts. 'Many fellows your age would jump at the chance. He must think you can do it. And you're interested in films. You're always at that cinema.'

Duncan wasn't a teenager's idea of a dynamic boss: middle-aged, balding, his roly-poly figure emphasized by the grocer's apron tied tightly round it; but he was a good man; and he'd told Andrew that he was the best delivery boy they had ever had, so he wasn't acting out of self-interest by advising him to take the job at the cinema.

'But I was planning to go into the Royal Air Force,' Andrew said.

Duncan looked at him for a long moment. He was a kind-hearted boss.

Andrew had known this shop since his mother first brought him here, soon after he was able to walk. There was something here than enthralled him when he was little. It was the print that Duncan Christie had on the wall above the counter. And it was still there, after all those years. It was a Highland regiment drummer in nineteenth century uniform. The composition of scarlet tunic, black busby and white cockade and kilt fascinated him. But it was the tenor drum that that riveted his attention. The honey-coloured casing, the white cords holding the drum-skin tight, the looped lanyard hanging down from it and the design of a pair of leopards on the drum side. And there was an association in his mind with the kilted figure and his memory image of a kilted man in khaki holding him and throwing him in the air, and catching him and throwing him in the air again. It was one of his earliest memories. His mother told him the soldier was his father.

'Well, quite a few fellows from around here have made careers in the services,' Duncan said thoughtfully. 'Your mother won't be happy though.'

Andrew shook his head, 'No, she's against it.'

Duncan nodded. It was time to lock up, and he switched off the lights in the front shop. 'You've a few days to talk about this offer with her.'

But talk it over with his mother was the last thing Andrew was going to do right now.

His plan had been straightforward. He would stay at school until the end of the school-year; in May he would sit the Leaving Certificate, which would help him rise to a higher rank in the RAF; he hoped to go into the wireless branch of the service. Meanwhile, he was content to work in his spare time, earning money as a delivery boy. He gave his pay over to his mother; he kept the tips he got for books, magazines and the cinema. And unlike some of his friends at school, he knew what he wanted to do with his future.

His father would have approved of his choice. At home they had a shining silver cup, a cup his father had been presented with. Its inscription read:

Private Iain Douglas,
1st Vol. Coy. Seaforth Highlanders,
SOUTH AFRICA. 1901-02

'Honor et Veritas.'

His father had only been nineteen when he volunteered for the South African war. And then,

17

although he was married with a young child, he had been called up in 1916 for the Great War. He would surely have been proud of his son entering the country's newest service.

It was all playing out according to the game plan, until the cinema manager put the ball up on the slates. Any other job offer and he would have been able to say no politely, and that would be the end of it. But it wasn't any job. It was this job, in the cinema.

He really loved film. The cinema showed three feature films a week, each playing for two nights. Films were not allowed to be shown on Sunday. He bought the American movie magazine *Photoplay* every month and read about the newest releases, so that he could keep up to date with what might be coming soon. The American director Raoul Walsh had made a western in 70mm. It was called *The Big Trail* and starred an unknown young actor in the lead, John Wayne. It had just been released in America at the beginning of the month. There was usually a time lag before American films reached Britain. But *All Quiet on the Western Front* had won Oscars this year, and it was being played this week. He'd read reviews; he had to see it.

But he had to think of tactics here. It would be best to say nothing to his mother about Stuart Robertson's offer until he knew whether she would let him see this film. There were problems though: the kind of film it was; and when it was being shown.

A war film was anathema to his mother. She might put her foot down; and he was boxed in when it came to options. Friday was the busiest day for grocery deliveries; he usually didn't finish until about 7pm, so it had to be the second house if he wanted to see the third film of the week. It had to be Friday.

His mother refused to allow him to go to the second house on a Saturday. It was taboo. A doctor, who had often been called on to put stitches in men's heads in the late hours, went on record in a local paper that the night before the Highland Sabbath the god Bacchus governed the streets.

According to the drinking laws, licensed premises had to close at 9pm. But up till that time the pubs did a roaring trade; then they abruptly turned their drinkers out on the stroke of the hour. If their doors were not closed by ten minutes after closing time, the publicans would fall foul of the law. The police patrolled the areas close to each pub, and enforced the law; they then strangely vanished before the storm broke. Pools of drunks, all men, who had tanked up quickly to beat the deadline, formed on the pavements and spilled over onto the streets, settling there for perhaps hours, slowly evaporating. Various moods prevailed, but only for a while, over the swaying groups: bursts of song were superseded by arguments; the world was put to rights; old grievances resurfaced, and there were frequent fistfights. It was like turbulence at sea, unpredictable, quick to change, and, like the forces of nature, uncontrollable. What was noticeable to the hardy individual going about his own business, hoping to pass by unnoticed in the shadows was that the drinkers who had served in the trenches were seldom aggressive; many veterans drank heavily and systematically on a Saturday night to get drunk, and drink themselves into oblivion. It was the younger men who were more likely to start fights. And passersby were at risk of being accosted and brought into a dispute. Saturday night on the streets of the small town from 9pm onwards was the dark side of an idyllic place to be brought up in.

He resolved on the way home that he would say nothing before his mother either allowed or forbade him to go to the war film on Friday. If she said no to it, he would spring the job offer on her, and announce he was going to take it; he would be working for a living, and he would see every film that played at the cinema.

But he couldn't concentrate at school on Thursday. It was worse at home. He picked up his father's silver cup from the dresser. The hallmark gave the name of the silversmith company and the city of manufacture: Sheffield, and in the reign of Edward VII. That was so long ago. His father would have been only four years older than he was now. With experience behind him, what would his father have said about his son's dilemma? *You're swithering. You're like a trout gliding along in a shady pool, jumping at the first fly that comes along.* Would he have taken a hectoring line? Or would he have discussed it quietly with him, guiding him but letting him make his own decisions?

He couldn't discuss it as a problem with his mother — that was for sure. It would be ding-dong, ding-dong all the way: no to the cinema job; no to the RAF, stay on at school. She wanted him to apply for a bursary for higher education. A year ago he had broached the idea of going into the Air Force under their Apprentice Scheme. The RAF were not keen to take on a boy without his parents' permission though; there was something about the spirit that they wanted to encourage in the service, the literature he'd sent for said. By next summer though, he would be a year older.

He felt his mother didn't know the wider world; she wasn't aware of the training opportunities that were available, where you could earn money as you trained. But it wasn't easy for him either: if he went into the forces, he would have a conscience about abandoning his mother, although money would be deducted from his service pay each week to be sent to her. On the other hand, if he took the cinema job . . .

John Cameron walked thoughtfully from the cinema to the church. He was in his early-forties, a little under six feet tall, of medium build with a firm jawline; his face was weathered from being out in all weathers most days. His dark hair was greying at the temples; and although it had been a frosty morning when he set out, he didn't have a coat: he wore a three piece, Prince of Wales tweed suit, not the funereal black habitually worn in public by clergymen of the time.

He wanted to think about the film he had just seen before he collected papers from the vestry for this evening's sub-committee meeting; he took a roundabout walk to the church. He had seen Charlie Chaplin films when he was a padre. It was laughter and a complete contrast to what they'd been through that the soldiers responded to, in jam-packed community halls in France.

He hadn't really known what to expect of this film. The subdued start was deceiving. His mind wandered to his own introduction to the war in France. He had been assigned to a forward field hospital, a church with part of the roof missing. No hospital he'd been to in civilian life disturbed him as much as this one did. They were all so young; and they were being maimed and killed in their thousands by the day.

Not long afterwards he was ordered to the front. He went out one night with a stretcher party to a salient that had been under constant attack for days. Steady rain was falling, as they made their way through mud; an occasional flare drooped lazily to earth. The stretcher bearers brought back the wounded and the dead. The survivors seemed dazed and deafened by what they had been through. He hadn't been able to come out with pious platitudes, 'We are in God's hands.' Instead he gave them cigarettes. They got comfort from a smoke, their soaking uniforms drying on them; and all around, the smell of death. The dugout was a charnel house.

And then the film began to bring back the nightmare. The battle scenes must have been arranged by someone with personal experience of artillery bombardment. The demented screaming of the shells on the soundtrack; the images of the barrage of heavy guns, tearing the earth asunder, as though a malevolent cosmic force was doing its worst to destroys mortals; the brief silence that followed; officers blowing whistles; then the gates of hell gaping open for them when the infantry climbed from their trenches and ran forward into withering fire from fixed gun positions.

He had known that fear they felt. It gripped him when he went over the top and ran more than fifty yards into the field of fire to lift a wounded man and carry him back to the lines. Miraculously, he had been almost unscathed; the first time he did it a bullet tore through his left shoulder epaulette and gouged his flesh. Undeterred he went again, and yet again. Altogether he brought back three wounded men, and he had received two flesh wounds. They had given him the Military Cross for bravery. Not that he gloried in the award. He'd saved three lives, and he was proud of that fact. Perhaps he had done more good as a padre saving three lives than he'd done in all his years as a clergyman in parish work.

It was not that he'd lost his basic belief, he told himself. There had to be a God. The natural world hadn't come about by random chance; there had to be intelligent design behind it. Man's mind, consciousness and moral understanding hadn't come about through evolution. Christian teachings were the highest good. But the war undermined his faith, and he'd been racked by doubts for years.

When Alice died he was twenty-five. Though he'd been devastated, he had been able, over time, to come to terms with his loss. They had met when they were both undergraduates. He then went to theological college; she trained as a teacher. They married, and she took a year out after teacher training to act as a volunteer with a social group working in the slums of Glasgow. She contracted the infectious disease diphtheria. After it was diagnosed, Alice was put into quarantine; he was only allowed to see her through a glass window — his wife. She suffered: the disease mercilessly gripped her, and she was in pain. As her condition worsened, he prayed for her to recover; and then he hoped that he would become infected too. Neither happened. She died within the year.

Even then, he hadn't let bitterness corrode his mind; he hadn't railed against God at the unfairness of her illness and death. He never lost his faith; he believed that there must be some divine reason behind it that he could never understand. And although she was dead, he was still in love with her; he couldn't see her but he felt she was close; his love for her kept her alive. No one would ever take her place.

Perhaps he'd been guilty of pride in thinking that his experience might qualify him to minister to soldiers when war came two years later.

After the first autumn offensive of the war, he became troubled in spirit. A sentimental myth had been put about in 1914 of the Angel of Mons in the sky, protecting British troops. Why British troops over German troops? Reality was very different.

He found he couldn't reconcile belief in a benevolent God with the scale of the slaughter on the Western Front. Why did Christ's blood not stream in the firmament above Passchendaele? Where was God at the Somme? Over a million casualties on all sides! Why had God not intervened in history? He knew the scholarly theological arguments against that kind of thinking; but when you saw for yourself the scraps of uniform adhering to the flesh of what had been men impaled for days on the barbed wire, and you were called on to identify the dead, your spirit rose in revolt.

The thought of God's indifference appalled him. Perhaps God had despaired of humankind, and left this planet untended, and gone on and created new and better worlds in limitless space. He'd mentally composed letters to Alice from the front and told her his fears.

As time flowed on though, memory began to shut down; a numbness settled on his spirit, and he went through the motions, without questioning himself; and so the intensity of his inner turmoil subsided. But the film rekindled it. And if he still felt like that, was it not dishonest to continue in his vocation? At forty-three he was probably too old to train as a school teacher. Perhaps he could apply for a job teaching comparative religion in a college. Perhaps he should just soldier on, humbly, and pray and hope. As he walked, he repeated to himself the words from Mark's gospel, 'I believe, help Thou mine unbelief.'

A coal lorry, that looked like an army surplus from the war, rattled slowly out of the lane leading to the rear of the church and the hall. There had been a delivery of coal for the furnace. He turned into the lane and walked towards the vestry. He could hear the rhythmic scraping of a shovel on flagstone. As he approached the church gable, Kenneth Grant, the church officer, was shovelling the load of fuel into the furnace room.

John watched in admiration, as he approached. The aperture in the wall of the furnace room, beside which the load of fuel had been tipped, could not have been more than eighteen inches by twelve inches. It required dexterity to achieve a swing with a shovel-load that minimized the demands on the arms and back muscles, and yet accurately delivered the contents into the small opening. Kennie had had mortar wounds to the shoulder during the war, but it didn't seem to impede the fluid two-part back and arms action. He'd once asked Kennie about when he'd been wounded, to be told, without much drama, 'It was at night out in no-man's land, with a small reconnaissance party, and one damn fool lit a cigarette.' And the mortar shell that wounded him killed the man beside him, a fellow townsman.

'Hello Kennie,' John said, announcing his presence.

Kennie put the blade of the shovel on the flagstone, and lifted the fingers of his right hand to his bonnet in the courteous salutation that went back to an earlier age, 'Fine morning.'

'Yes, indeed it is. I came round to the vestry to collect papers for the presbytery sub-committee tonight.' John said. 'It's at 7.30pm. But don't bother coming in especially for that Kennie. There will only be the three of us. I'll let myself and the others in by the side-door.'

'I'll leave the gas fire in the vestry on at a low setting this afternoon.' Kennie paused, and emphasized his words, 'You'll remember to turn it off when you're finished?'

'Yes, I'll try and remember,' and he laughed and left him to it. John had warmed to the kind of man Kennie was from the beginning: he was a man of few words, but a thoughtful man. In his early fifties, he had been church officer for twenty years.

When he had collected the papers he'd come for, John Cameron left the church to walk to the manse. His housekeeper, Mrs Mackenzie, would be preparing lunch. He greeted passers-by and shoppers; but when he left the area where there were shops, he found a tune was running through his head. It was one of those annoying things, where he knew the tune but couldn't place it, couldn't identify it. Maybe it was one of those revivalist happy little melodies. Then a broad smile lit his face. It certainly wasn't a revivalist hymn; it was 'Mademoiselle from Armentières', one of the most popular songs of the war at the front. And he ran over the tune and the words of the first verse in his mind, as he walked:

'Mademoiselle from Armentières,
Parlez- vous,
Mademoiselle from Armentières,
Parlez-vous.'

Why on earth had a rude song from the war come to mind? And then it dawned upon him: of course, it was the film, the scene where three or four German soldiers swim across the river to an inn and spend the night with some French girls. And without conscious effort the appropriate verse came back to him, prompted by the warm human scene in the film, and he sang softly to himself,

'Three German officers crossed the Rhine,
Parlez-vous,
Three German officers crossed the Rhine,

27

Parlez-vous,
Three German officers crossed the Rhine,
To fuck the women and drink the wine,
Hinky-dinky parlez-vous.'

The tune had a catchy rhythm that invited a
quick-change of step at the end of each verse.
Along the road he went; and, lighter in heart, he
executed a final quick-change of step and a smart
left turn and went into the driveway to the manse.

In a small town with a long history you usually find
a group who are its oral chroniclers. Tain,
however, the oldest Royal Burgh in Scotland,
birthplace of a saint of the Celtic Church and once
an important pilgrimage site for kings of Scotland,
had two such groups, with complementary, rather
than overlapping, roles.

The pre-eminent of the two groups, in their
own eyes, were the Worthies. They were all men.
They met only in the open air. And there were faint
echoes of the peripatetic school of philosophers
about them — although the Worthies'
peregrinations were circumscribed to the
pavements of the High Street: the south side at the
junction of King Street or Market Street; or its
north side, at the Kenneth Murray memorial.

Membership was not confined to particular
rungs on the social ladder. None of them was
devoutly religious. Nor were they antagonistic to
organized religion. They appeared to be the
inheritors of a tradition of freethinkers.

These record-keepers of the burgh were
concerned with the broad sweep of the year's

events in relation to past years, and to the town's development: the commercial concerns which were superseded or went under in the last thirty years. They gave some provisional thought to this new picture show in the old Town Hall; it was an advance on the travelling shows of Pinder Ord; it was permanent, intended to give entertainment over a wide age range; and it gave some local employment, at a time when work was hard to come by.

They were not concerned with the peccadilloes of their fellow townspeople; when they did discuss an individual, it was generally whimsically and with respect, for he was already in the grave.

But their counterparts were another cup of tea altogether. They were the Clashbags. It was a Scots word, meaning chatter or gossip. They were usually referred to in the collective as the Clash, but the term Clashbag applied to the individual. Unlike the Worthies, the Clash comprised both men and women. They were not confined when it came to meeting places: wherever two or three were gathered together, no matter in whose name, or for whatever purpose, they were active. But unlike the Worthies, the Clash were very much concerned with their fellow townspeople.

Clash veterans were a *corps d'élite*, they were the shock troops of story-spinning, with a shoot-to-kill policy, establishing bridgeheads for others to develop. A seasoned Clashbag was a sharp-shooter when it came to taking out a character.

'Cameron the minister's raving mad. Skipping along the road to the manse like a spring lamb, singing hymns at the pitch of his voice.'

'His bosom pal is that godless conchie, the manager of that cinema.'

'And now his head's full o' magic lanterns.'

'He's away with it completely.'

"That's why his wife left him.'

'Isn't he a widower?'

'We don't know the half of it. What woman could live with that?'

'They'll need to get rid of him.'

'He'll be in the loony bin before that happens.'

If Saturday night after nine o'clock was the dark side of the ancient burgh, at all hours, the Clash were its sinister grey, while the Worthies blended with its mellow sandstone buildings.

Later that night, frost set in again. Stuart left the cinema by the side door, well pleased with Friday's attendances. The first house was three-quarters full, the second house packed out. Some customers had to be turned away. On Saturday, it would no doubt play to full houses.

It was a little after eleven pm. He crossed the street, and stood for a moment looking at the darkened frontage of the building. It was well-named, Town Hall Cinema; built over fifty years ago, it was a far cry from the purpose-built cinemas of the large towns and cities. Yet, he had grown attached to it.

His breath, turning into condensation, formed white cones momentarily in the air, then disappeared. He set off for his accommodation. When he came to the town, he'd taken a room; his landlady supplied breakfast each day and lunch on

Sunday, and he made his own arrangements with the hotel beside the cinema for the rest of his meals.

Tonight, however, he took a detour from his usual route so that he would pass by the house of Linda Graham. Her husband, who had been a lot older than her, had died several years ago. He'd come from a well-to-do family, and he had left his widow well provided for, with the stipulation that she didn't remarry. In that event — so the Clash had it — her share of the trust fund would revert to his spinster sister. Linda Graham did not lament her lot, but learned to live with it very successfully. She became a discreet merry widow. Stuart had met her at a charity lunch in the Royal Hotel. He estimated that she was on the wrong side of forty-five, but she had a good appearance; she was an alert and self-confident woman who kept her matronly shape fit on the golf course, and she entertained from time to time.

She had taken him to her bed on two evenings already after he had left the cinema. He'd stayed for some time, slinking away in the early hours of the morning, in the hope that he wouldn't be seen. The signal she had pre-arranged with him was quite simple and not open to ambiguity: Friday night was a good night for him to call in late, provided that her sister-in-law hadn't come visiting for the week-end. The lights in the large conservatory at the back of Linda's house would be on, but if the blind on the window to the right of the conservatory door was pulled down, she was alone and able to receive him.

He turned into the street where she lived. As he got nearer her house, he saw that the blind was down. Automatically, he put on a spurt to his pace lest the light go out, crossed the street, and stepped on to the pavement. There was no one in sight; he turned the wrought iron gate handle.

He pressed the doorbell. After half a minute Linda appeared from the main part of the house, saw who it was, unlocked the outer door and opened it.

'Come in stranger. It's been a while,' she said.

He smiled as he wiped his feet on the mat, 'The old story. No rest for the wicked,' he said. 'Not able to get away from work before some ungodly hour.'

She simply smiled and led the way. He admired her strength of character. She had no more deep feelings for him than she had for anyone else she may have invited; she'd conditions imposed on her; she got round them in her way, and made a life for herself. She was her own person.

When Andrew broke the news at home on Saturday evening that he was going to leave school at Christmas and work in the cinema, there was a family row the like of which they hadn't had for more than two years.

He had been allowed to go to see *All Quiet on the Western Front* on Friday; and there was a scene in the film that tipped the balance for him in favour of working in the cinema. It was the scene where the young hero, Paul, home on convalescent leave after being wounded, returns to visit his old school, the building he left to become a soldier. His old teacher urges him to say a few words to the senior boys, to fire them with enthusiasm to serve their country. Paul, having gone through the hell of trench warfare, at first says that he can't tell them anything, but as the teacher persists, Paul realizes the doddering codger is still spouting to the boys *Dulce et decorum est pro patria mori* (it is sweet and seemly to die for one's country). Paul loses his cool, and tells the boys that it is better not to die for your country; and he storms out of the school.

That scene winded him; it was a blow to the guts: the real meaning behind his father's military service record dawned on him. It was there all the time but he hadn't wanted to see it. Yes, his father had left home and gone to war; the first time he was only nineteen; but he must have learned his lesson, because the second time, he didn't volunteer, he had to be conscripted; the Great War was two years old when the government brought in conscription — he had been forced to serve. Andrew had been wrong in automatically assuming his father would have been proud of him for choosing the armed forces for a career. He might well have advised against it.

And so he now thought about his options differently. He could choose a service career if that's where his real interest lay; or he could choose film exhibition because he loved film.

It didn't take him long to decide. He would take the cinema job.

He had Saturday at work to think about tactics for the confrontation with his mother. Although it was always a busy day and he didn't have much time on his own, there was one delivery on a

Saturday he normally dreaded, but it gave him the time to think. It was a run to a house three miles from the town; for the last mile he had to leave the road and cycle mostly uphill along a steep farm track. All the weight of the heavy basket of groceries in the deep metal framework of the specially adapted bike pressed down on the smaller front wheel. He had to rise high off the seat to force the pedals down for each revolution. He took in breath in big gulps; his heart was pumping; he felt as though blood was being forced up into his throat. But this huge effort worked wonders for the brain: inspiration came to him. He would play his part for the showdown as though he was working from a film script.

Freewheeling on the downhill return run, he whizzed along, wind in his face at a stomach-tingling speed, rehearsing his lines.

'You're not leaving school.'

'I'm leaving, I've made my mind up.'

His mother looked at him in disbelief. 'I've tried to do my best for you on my own. I don't know what I've done wrong.'

'You haven't done anything wrong. It's my life, my choice.'

Variations of these exchanges continued for a little while, but brought them no closer to a resolution. Then his mother ratcheted the tension up a notch by giving way to a flood of tears. But he didn't dissolve, and give in, as he had in the past, when she cried. Hollywood scriptwriters didn't let a film's leading men give in to women's tears; they gave them snappy one or two-word comments; dialogue was pared down to the essentials, and that way was more effective. And he could see the realisation on his mother's part that the old tactics weren't working any more.

It excited him to see that what he'd picked up from films could be applied in real life. He was aware, ever since the cinema opened in the town, that some of his friends at school were aping words and expressions of American English they got from films. Instead of falling into the slow, laconic speech of the older generation, they were going in for quick-fire dialogue and American slang. The change in their speech-patterns in the short time was noticeable. Before the cinema came, BBC radio transmissions only just reached this part of the world; and before that all they had were the newspapers and the Carnegie Library. But now they could go to the 'talkies.'

He'd played his part cannily since Stuart Robertson spoke to him on Wednesday. When his mother angrily demanded why he hadn't told her ut the cinema manager's offer earlier, he craftily brought it round to his need of a few days to make up his own mind first.

'You're headstrong.'

'Isn't that a good thing so you're not pushed around easily by people.'

This exasperated her, and she lapsed into silence. Her brows were knit in a heavy frown. Andrew said nothing more. He knew it would be a mistake for him to talk too much. He had to let it come from her; and he had to respond to each point, keeping a cool head. In this way a heavy cloud of gloom gathered, then settled over the living-room for the rest of the evening.

The cloud had not lifted overnight But his mother observed a silent truce while they got ready to attend the Remembrance ceremonies.

After the church service came the final part of the Remembrance ceremony, the laying of wreaths at the war memorial in front of the Tolbooth to whose wall the Seaforth memorial was attached. Dense crowds lined both sides of the High Street.

To the east, lost from sight by the buildings on the High Street, and heralding a change in the weather, a watery-looking sun with mares' tails of cloud athwart it hung low in the sky. Stuart Robertson stood far back on the south pavement. He thought back to the cheering crowds of 1914, the war fever, bellicose headlines; the taunting if you thought differently; then the drumming at the hands of the tribunal, men patriotic, indifferent to principle; three months in prison; agreeing to be an 'alternativist', unloading ships in the dockyard.

From the east marched the parade led by the pipes and drums in the Red Ross tartan, playing a medley of retreat airs: 'The Green Hills of Tyrol' and 'When the Battle's O'er.' Helen Ross was composed and dignified as she led the Girl Guide contingent; she gave herself up to her duties as captain, anxious that the girls comport themselves well, and kept in step with the slower pace of the pipe band. When the parade was all in place at the memorial, the Provost, on behalf of the Town Council, laid a wreath, followed by the Commanding Officer of the military detachment and then the British Legion.

Andrew noticed his mother's fingers tighten their hold on her handbag at the first piercing notes of the piper's lament, 'The Flowers of the Forest'. Nothing stirred. No one moved. Then two buglers sounded 'Last Post', followed by the silence, and the playing of 'Reveille'. And the ceremony ended.

Andrew and his mother walked home in silence. And it was not because they'd been rowing the evening before; they had their own thoughts. As soon as they were in the house, and before his mother took off her hat and coat, she said, 'I want you to ask the cinema manager to write to the rector of the academy and request that you are allowed to sit your exams in May. It wouldn't interfere with working in the evening. I'll write to the rector as well, and ask him.' She paused, and waited for his response. But before he could make it, she continued. 'Having a certificate would be something to fall back on if you ever change jobs.'

She'd thought about it during the night, and the Remembrance ceremonies reinforced it for her: she had lost a husband to a war he hadn't volunteered for; she didn't want to drive a son into the Armed Forces for ten years when who knew what lay ahead.

He was completely taken aback. He was taller than his mother now. She looked worn-out. She had always tried to do her best for him. He wanted to put his arm round her and protect her. He was the man now; he would make his own decisions. He had won. But film scenarios hadn't prepared him for total victory, only for the fight. So he just nodded, and said, 'All right.'

At two pm that afternoon, Helen met her friend Joyce at the academy gates, and they went on a Sunday stroll; as the light would go early, they chose a short walk along the north road out of the town. The road ran parallel with the firth.

Joyce had been in the same year as Helen at school. She was slightly shorter than her, with fair hair that framed a heart-shaped face. She worked in a dress shop on the High Street; she was always nicely turned out.

'How about going to see the Greta Garbo film that's on Monday and Tuesday?' Helen asked.

'You don't go the pictures,' Joyce said in surprise. 'What's happened?'

'I know, but the way the minister spoke about that film in the service. It made me think some of them might be worth seeing,' Helen said.

'It was moving the way he put it.'

'Two girls at the Guides on Friday were talking about the Greta Garbo film, *Anna Christie*.'

'Why not? We could go tomorrow night.'

'Yes, that would be good.'

They had been best friends for about ten years now. Joyce was single as well and very aware of the shortage of eligible, unattached men in the area. She sometimes shared her thoughts with Helen whenever a commercial traveller she liked the look of visited the shop, although she was generally wary of the breed.

'The picture house manager looks quite good in his penguin suit, standing at the top of the steps,' Joyce said.

'He seems all right,' Helen said. She'd heard some of the gossip that follows in the trail of a newcomer, and she was non-committal.

Strangely, most recently, it was Helen who had been sought after by a man. Only two years ago, a local farmer, a heavy-set and slowly-spoken widower in his forties, had proposed marriage to her. He had made the offer to her in her office when he was in to meet David Sangster in connection with the purchase of some acres of land from a neighbouring farmer. He'd asked her in all seriousness as she was working at her desk.

'Would you like to move in wi' me; be the wife like? The farmhouse has a grand kitchen wi' a Raeburn.'

She realized to her horror that this was a proposal of marriage. It was as if he was doing a business deal, offering a bit of grazing land in exchange for a heifer. She burst out laughing. And instantly saw from his eyes that he was hurt. She tried at once to mitigate what she'd done; she put the absurdity of it on to herself. 'I'm hopeless in a kitchen. I can't cook.' He was not taken in, however; he said nothing, and turned towards the door; he lowered his head, and, as he turned the door handle, it seemed his spine had caved in on him. Bovine he may have appeared to be, but he had feelings; and she'd wounded him deeply.

When she'd told Joyce about the proposal of marriage in her office while she worked, she made a joke of it. 'Imagine typing up a Confirmation of Estate form on behalf of a client. You're in the middle of a paragraph on page two, the door opens, and without more ado, this big ox comes in and he proposes to you — in his own way.

'He didn't come out with sweet nothings?'

'Said he had a good Raeburn cooker.'

'Fancy wakening in the morning and finding that Romeo in bed next to you,' Joyce teased, with tears of laughter running down her face.

Once they left the shelter of buildings, the Dornoch Firth lay grey and cheerless to their right. The hills of Sutherland were shrouded in mist, and the sea and the sky were sombre grey. There was no traffic and there were no other walkers on the road. Today they were going to turn at the massive stone by the roadside, which was inscribed with the words 'The Immortal Walter Scott, OB 1832'.

They walked in silence. Helen's thoughts drifted to the Remembrance service, to the image of the trenches and the butterfly; the walk with Alan that day long ago in late spring.

By three pm that afternoon, the sky was closing in. From the perspective of its southern shore, with the tide far out, the Dornoch Firth was a leaden valley-floor, draining the Sutherland hills. A light wind heralding rain in its wake blew softly from the west.

Stuart approached the narrow suspension footbridge at the mouth of the river. He crossed it, balancing each step, trying to anticipate the swaying cables' reaction; then he began walking along the shoreline. There was no other living soul on the beach.

At one point he had to come off the dunes and walk on the sand from where the tide had ebbed. He continued along the widening firth line. The North Sea, obedient to the laws of the universe, had retreated; there was mysterious order and harmony governing its movements. After another half mile, he came across the bleached trunk of a mature tree with one bough and a few straggly stumps of branches. The trunk had been plaything to the tides of ages, until, tiring of it, they finally beached it. Strands of sea wrack were entwined round its branches, as though left in a gap-toothed comb by a weird sea goddess; and the distant strip of water was a grey ribbon she'd dropped far out, near the horizon.

The Gizzen Briggs, a bridge of sand, stretched towards the north, creating the illusion for a few hours that you could walk across; but the tide would return and reclaim the firth.

You could be deceived about where you were in life too, he felt. Your perspective changed over time he'd found. Sunday School's God had given way to faith in human reason; and that seeped away during the war. Now, thirty-five: halfway through the biblical three score and ten. Perhaps it was a sense of responsibility that bore in on him; this was his first cinema. He would like to go further though, be responsible for a city's big prestigious theatre. He had striven, and he had succeeded. But at a cost.

It was really no life this, on your own in your mid-thirties. All right in your twenties. He wished he had someone he loved. What a difference that would make! He almost had it once, sixteen years ago, until her father forbade her to continue seeing a coward who wasn't prepared to fight for his country. Not that there was a dearth of young women in the town, but of those he'd watched filing past the box office, none strongly appealed to him. Linda wasn't an answer. She was available, that was all. He rigorously sifted women into two categories: those he knew at once he couldn't relate to emotionally; and those he found himself drawn to from the start. He didn't accept that loving someone came about through a kind of osmosis; it was electric energy. You knew soon after meeting her whether you could or couldn't love her.

Helen Ross came to his mind. He'd seen her walking along Tower Street to work. Then this morning he'd observed her during the service as she sat with the Girl Guides in the church, and he saw her in the parade. She had fine features; she held herself well; her dark hair was done up under the uniform hat. But how to meet her? He'd never seen her at the cinema. She seemed reserved.

His mind drifted again, back to last night. The cinema staff included a doorman in green livery and he shepherded the queue for each house. But when a really popular film was being shown and the length of the queue was such that all seats for the second house would be sold out, leaving some customers disappointed, Stuart felt it was good management practice if he himself walked long the queue, doing a mental count. When he came to that point where there was no hope of the rest being admitted, he told them. But he assured them that he would try and bring back the film.

And it was that niggling incident of last night and his over-reaction to it that he wanted to walk off. It still riled him that his normally light-footed response deserted him in a flash of anger. He had just turned his back on that part of the queue that was unlikely to gain admission, and he began to walk towards the cinema steps when faintly audible came, 'Bloody conchie!' from a youth in his late teens or early twenties, who was with two friends, an insolent smirk still lingering on his face. Instead of nimbly side-stepping the taunt or pretending he hadn't heard and allowing the youth to feel a sense of bravado among his friends, Stuart rounded on him, 'Keep a civil tongue, or you'll be barred from the cinema for good.' He could have kicked himself. Other customers had witnessed it; at once there was that tense hush that follows confrontation when someone either loses face or resorts to violence. He had reverted; he'd forgotten he no longer rang a leper's bell; he wasn't shunned any more. Public feeling had changed, and cadres of young men at the universities were vociferous in proclaiming anti-war sentiments. Of course he couldn't be expected to accept abuse from a member of the public, queuing for the cinema, but he could have handled it differently. And it irked him.

The truth was he was frazzled. You're always the last to see it in yourself though. He'd been overworking; he hadn't had a break for the past two years. He was too close to the job, he couldn't stand back from it. And his work isolated him. It contributed to his over-working. Certainly, he had a lot of social contact, but he was at work and the customers were enjoying their leisure time; and when he was free, they were at work. It had been less noticeable when he worked in Glasgow: the bustle and activity of the city was absorbing. But in a small town he felt his isolation more. That was something he knew he had in common with John Cameron: both lived lonely lives; though in John's case, he knew because John had told him, it was choice after his wife died; but he, Stuart, wished he had a life partner. He liked talking with John; he felt that he was a kindred spirit; he suspected that, like himself, John had lost, or at least had difficulty in holding onto his early beliefs; and it was because of the war. What were the final words of the prologue to *All Quiet on the Western Front*? He closed his eyes, and tried to recall them: a generation of men, 'who, even though they may have escaped its shells, were destroyed by the war.' That applied not only to soldiers.

Ahead of him, camouflaged against the sand and busily intent at a pool the tide had left behind when it ebbed, was a solitary curlew; its hooked bill, rising and falling as it fed, was the only movement that gave away its presence. Suddenly, it rose in the air shrieking its *whaup* of alarm.

He'd been away so long that the light was fading when he stepped on to the suspension bridge across the river on his way back to town. As the last gentle undulation of the bridge evened out, his eyes were drawn through the veil of fine rain towards the ruin of St Duthac Chapel. What power was once perceived to lie here with the relics of a saint when kings of Scotland came on pilgrimage?

On a whim, he turned left and walked along to the gates of the cemetery and went in. He made for the ruined chapel on the knoll. The ivy leaves on its walls flicked back and forth noiselessly, slicked by the slanting drizzle. Whatever potency may once have resided here had long gone; all that moved now was powered by the wind. And the cemetery was left to the dead.

After he'd structured his sermon for the evening service, John Cameron put on his coat and went out into the manse grounds to rinse his mind and for a change of scene. On Sundays his housekeeper worked until two in the afternoon, and he prepared his own evening meal. A light rain was falling. It was a little after five. The manse stood on high ground, on what had had been the shoreline millions of years ago; it overlooked part of the town but also gave a sweeping vista across the firth; but now the distant hills were obscured.

His thoughts drifted. The artifice of film brought it all back to him. He'd fallen into the slough of despond, and there, gradually, his emotions hibernated as the traumatic years receded. But his response to Lewis Milestone's war film awakened them and left him again at the mercy of his worst doubts. At the Remembrance service he had spoken from the heart, not from orthodox Christianity; and it had left him emotionally drained. He stood for a while and tried to restore himself as darkness fell.

Later, with the by now steady drizzle blowing in his face, John was still in sombre mood as he walked to conduct the evening service.

The gas fire in the vestry purred out its welcoming warmth. After a few minutes, there was a knock at the vestry door, and the session clerk came in. He was in his early sixties. He had a distinguished-looking head, with a high forehead and silver hair brushed back. He still worked as a farm grieve, the overseer of farmhands. 'Could you spare a few minutes in the session room after the service? Willie Meikle's on his high horse again. Something about desecration,' and here the session clerk feigned gravity, 'in the very House of the Lord on the Sabbath.'

'What's he on about this time?'

'You'd better come and listen to him. He's on about magic lanterns. Maybe you can humour him.'

Willie Meikle was in his late-forties, diminutive in height, and he strained to make up in sagacity and spiritual muscle what he lacked in stature. For a man of his height and leg length, he walked with a ridiculous gait, taking long strides, as though he wore the seven-league boots. John Cameron considered him the Cassandra of the kirk session, punctuating his discourse with the occasional Gaelic expression for exceptional gravity — a real pain in the arse. He had a small china shop in the town. He had been medically unfit for military service, and interpreted that as the Almighty's way of sparing him from the war in order that he could carry out spiritual work in the parish.

In every group where power is shared there are factions or in-groups; and kirk sessions are no exception. Willie had the distinction of being in a faction of one. He never tried to win over others. He might have resented it if they had joined him.

For he had been conditioned to being a loner. In his childhood years, as he continually failed to measure up with the growth spurts of his peers, his parents increasingly cosseted him. Until they set him on the pathway into a small business. As a result, he missed out on experiencing the intense emotional attachments in adolescence that nature urges us into. And he came to develop strength in his solitude, and adopted positions of absolute certainty on many of the vexed issues of life.

A small group of six elders gathered in the session room. The chairs were arranged in rows, facing the table where the session clerk and the minister sat. The session clerk's style was brisk. He nodded to the elder sitting nearest it to close the door. Then he gestured to Willie, 'What is it you want to bring up?'

Willie didn't speak immediately, he began by shaking his head slowly once or twice for theatrical effect. '*Ochoin, ochoin* (woe, woe). Magic lanterns spoken of in a Sabbath sermon in the House of the Lord. It's sacrilege. The Devil's work, and you enlarged on it in the morning service,' he said, pointing at the minister.

'That's nonsense! Films aren't the Devil's work. They're a form of art.'

'Abomination of images,' retorted Willie.

'Abomination your backside. They're pictures of ordinary people, played at speed through a projector,' said John warming to his task. The session clerk, with his management experience as

47

grieve on a large farm, was relishing the minister's robust language; it was a style of engagement he was used to at work. 'We're all of us here, elders,' continued John, 'and I'm the teaching elder, according to our Presbyterian form of church government. I decide what I include in my sermons, not you,' he said, pointing to Wille. 'And if you want to challenge it, I'll draft a letter to the presbytery clerk and have him put the challenge up to the General Assembly.'

At this, Willie's body language told the meeting he was wobbly; he was off-balance. This time he had taken too wide a step for his leg-reach. With a weaker minister, he might have succeeded by bluff. But he was suddenly vulnerable. And he knew it. Finding himself in a minority of one was no new experience for him, and he could even adapt it to his own ends. But a public rebuke from the national level of the church would bring local humiliation. The session clerk had difficulty in concealing his pleasure at Willie's discomfiture.

'Alternatively,' John went on, 'I'll make arrangements with the cinema manager for you to have a private viewing of a film in the cinema in the course of the week. You'll be able to see for yourself that film can be a medium for good.' He waited. No one spoke. And Willie squirmed.

'Well it's up to you. I'm prepared for both courses of action.'

'Aye, aye, it might not be a bad thing to see that magic lantern. Confront it with righteousness.'

The session clerk smartly swung back into his role as chairman again, 'That's settled then,' and concluded the meeting.

Prompted, under cover of darkness by the latest intelligence, a little after eight on Monday morning, the Clash established another bridgehead.

'They'll have to get rid of Cameron. He's gone beyond it this time.'

'You never heard the like of it. He swore like a trooper at Willie Meikle. He gave him a mouthful in the church.'

'And now he's going off to that cinema yet again. And he's forcing that godly man Willie to go as well. What's going on in that place?'

'They'll have to close it. Cameron'll have to go.'

Under the bright downlights of the foyer, the doorman's uniform glowed like a Halloween costume, as Helen joined the file of customers moving towards the cashier's box. She had come to the film on her own. Joyce had dashed from her shop on the High Street the few hundred yards to Helen's office at about three in the afternoon with the news that she had been asked to work late that night at an inventory for stocktaking; she had a choir practice on Tuesday; she was sorry about it, but . . . Helen had arranged with her mother that she wouldn't be home until 7.45 that evening, so she decided to go on her own.

She paid for her ticket and made her way towards the door of the stalls. The usher tore the ticket in half, and she was about to walk on when Stuart Robertson in evening suit came out of the

49

projection box. At once he smiled and said, 'I hope you enjoy the film.'

She gave him a smile in response and continued into the theatre to find a seat. It was surprising how many people were in the cinema. A few years ago she had seen a silent film when a travelling cinema company came to the town. It had been a distraction for the time it lasted, but nothing of it stayed with her afterwards; she had had no interest in repeating the experience until yesterday at the service.

The house lights dimmed; the trailer for a forthcoming film ran; then the credits for *Anna Christie* came up. Cigarette smoke swirls rose, lazily changing form, drifting across the beam of bright light, wraiths attending the magic lantern.

Then the cigarette smoke, caught in the light, blended with thick mist on the screen drifting over the surface of the water. Sounds of activity on New York's East River and the city beyond came as a surprise to her. So this was a 'talkie'.

Gradually, the scenes drew Helen into the story of Anna Christie, a young woman who wants to start a new life by returning to her father, skipper of a coal barge. When she was a child he had left her to be brought up by relatives; as a girl she escaped from an abusive situation; then hints that she went from the frying pan to the fire. But the story moved on, and Anna falls in love with a sailor; she feels she has to tell him about her dark past when she had to work in a house of ill-repute. She has the courage to do it. At first, the sailor can't cope with the reality; finally she finds happiness through love.

As Helen made her way along the stalls aisle towards the exit, filing out with the crowd, the contrast with her own life came to mind: the character was escaping from an awful past, whereas she escaped into her past, fondly envisioning times with Alan.

She spoke to a former Girl Guide and her boyfriend, who were coming out of a row nearer the back of the stalls. They moved with the crowd towards the exit. She had reached the foyer, and was a few paces short of the outside door, when the cinema manager, standing to the left in the foyer, made eye contact and with a graceful body movement skilfully interposed himself between her and those around her without getting in anyone else's way, speaking to her as he moved.

'Did you enjoy it?'

She blushed, then quickly composed herself and smiled, 'Yes, I liked it. Perhaps a bit stilted at times.' She felt like adding a reservation.

'What did you think of Greta Garbo?'

'She has a strong presence.'

'She was nominated for an Academy Award for the part.'

Without her really being aware of it, he was moving along with her and they were on the outside landing. Others round about could hear what they were saying, but he was in control and relaxed, as he gestured her to the left, in front of the display panels on the wall, so that the departing customers were not impeded.

'Although she was nominated for one, she didn't get the Oscar.'

It appeared to be effortless with him; this was his domain, and he had contrived that they were face to face and talking, and she didn't feel it had been forced or artificial.

'I've seen you walking to work. But I haven't seen you at the cinema before. I was hoping you might come one evening,' Stuart said.

Helen laughed, her eyes shone, 'I went once when the travelling show came. Didn't make much of an impression.'

'We have one or two interesting films about women with strong personalities in the next few weeks. You would like them.'

Helen was aware that the retreating file of customers from the first house was thinning down to a few stragglers, and those queuing below on the pavement, looking up at them, must soon be allowed to come up the steps.

Stuart Robertson was in charge though; he would give the signal to the doorman to bring the queue forward, 'Would you like to go for afternoon tea next Sunday? The Royal Hotel, three o'clock?'

She flushed a little, 'Yes,' she nodded, conscious of the crowd standing impatient down below them. 'Yes, all right,' she smiled.

'I'll meet you in the hotel foyer,' and he stood aside as she made her way down the flight of steps. Then he nodded to the doorman, who stood at the head of the file.

As she walked home, Helen tried to understand what had happened to her, she was confused. She'd blushed when he first spoke to her, for the moment he did so a scornful thought flashed through her mind: *You were safe and sound in the war.* A deeply buried prejudice she didn't even know she had had against wartime pacifists forced itself into her consciousness. At once, she felt ashamed. But she'd been flustered though, not only because of that first response, but also because, as they talked, she felt attracted to him: he exuded something; she couldn't pinpoint what, but she responded to him. Nothing like this had happened to her for years. She felt bewildered.

The following evening, the two women sat by the fireside. Helen's mother was knitting a Fair Isle pattern jersey; the steady rhythm of the needles was unbroken except when she nudged the wool away from its ball. Helen had the *Scotsman* crossword she'd begun in the office at lunchtime. The wind had got up in intensity, late in the afternoon, and now it roared in the chimney. Helen lifted her eyes from the crossword and looked into the fire. A hurdy-gurdy of emotions had been churning inside her for the past twenty-four hours: reawakened feelings and desire. Then there were moments of calm reasoning: she had been precipitate; she should have said no.

The coals glowed brightly as the wind drew air into the chimney vent. She thought about her life.

She had always lived here, this house that her great grandfather built in 1860. It represented stability to her grandparents, and they anticipated this would continue. But her mother's life had been turned upside down; and her own hadn't panned out as she thought when she was a girl. She had wanted to stay on at school and go to university.

'Stuart Robertson, the cinema manager, asked me to have tea with him on Sunday in the Royal.'

'And what did you say to him?'

'I said I would. But I'm thinking about changing my mind.'

'You should go. He seems a nice man.'

Helen lowered her eyes to the crossword.

They had grown into a companionable unit over the past ten years, she and her mother. But Helen had aged before her time. And yet, within the last day, long-dead feelings re-emerged. She hadn't imagined this would happen to her.

The wind, gusting in from the sea, howled in fury over the rooftops, as if to wrench the chimney from its housing. Between the gusts' ferocity could be heard the continual growling of the waves, savaging the Gizzen Briggs.

Stuart Robertson was looking for a mate. He was an incomer. He was not necessarily settled here. Then her thoughts turned to her mother: she was sixty-one, and coped very well, but in the future she would become more dependent. Yet, she herself had her own life to lead.

She found herself comparing him to Alan. There wasn't much difference in height, and they were both slim and dark haired. She had only one photo of Alan in uniform, taken on his last leave. He had a warm personality, and was kind and sensitive. But she'd known him from school days. This man! She stopped short. There was almost a generation's difference between the two men — she'd been clinging to a memory, to an image from the past.

Each gust of wind reached a new crescendo; the flames flared when drawn into the chimney vent.

Her mother raised her eyes, pausing the rhythm of the knitting needles; she looked into the fire, watching the coals glow in response to the surge of air; then, after the gust died back, a drifting spiral of smoke hovered aimlessly in the grate; she wondered for a moment might she, like her mother before her, succumb, in the end, to dementia's embrace. 'It's really wild tonight,' she said, looking at her daughter, 'I hope we don't lose any slates.'

'We had the roof checked over last year,' Helen said, and turned her eyes back to the crossword, but her mind was elsewhere. When she was in her early twenties she'd been bitter. There had been two men at different times who tried to court her; but she'd rejected them at the first advance. Bitterness had left its mark, and she wondered if it had soured her. Girls ten years younger than her were having families. But she belonged to the lost generation. She'd thought she would never alter the even tenor of her ways. But now her feelings were telling her something else.

She decided to stop agonizing. She'd said she'd meet him. And she would. She would take one step.

The tiled foyer was freshly mopped and dried; the pot plant had been dusted; and a cleaner had been primed to keep a look-out for Willie Meikle. Punctually, at nine-thirty on Thursday morning, Willie climbed the cinema steps, holding the handrail and carrying himself with dignity.

Stuart Robertson met him at the top, and greeted him. 'Come along. We're ready to begin. Is this your first time here?'

'No, I've been here when it was the Town Hall,' Willie said.

Stuart led the way to the left hand door into the stalls, 'I think you'll like this film. It doesn't have sound. Quite a lot of films now have sound, but this one hasn't.'

Willie shrugged his shoulders, as if to say it was immaterial to him; he was there under duress.

'Where would you like to sit?'

After looking around for a moment, Willie opted for a seat half way down the hall. Stuart nodded to George, who was in the projection box.

'I've things to see to, but I'll come back and join you later,' Stuart said, as the lights dimmed. The curtains opened, and he left Willie in the theatre.

'Keep an eye open in case he walks out,' Stuart said to George from the bottom step of the projection box; then he went to his office.

He had been surprised when John Cameron appeared at the cinema on Monday morning with the request that he put on a showing for 'this thorn in my flesh' as John described this morning's visitor. And he outlined the choice he'd given Willie. Time was of the essence, John explained, or he would have to write to the presbytery clerk, claiming an elder was challenging his status.

As it turned out, Thursday morning was the only time that week, Willie could leave his shop unattended for an hour and a half.

'Well,' Stuart said with a grimace, 'in that case there might be a problem. Our film for Thursday is *Pandora's Box* directed by a European, Georg Pabst. It stars Louise Brooks. The danger is Willie may be offended because she plays the part of

Lulu, a prostitute. On the other hand, for all this fellow's surface piety, deep down he's maybe a lecher. He might be charmed.'

'I hope you're right. If he's outraged, it'll reinforce his antagonism.'

Conscious that the outcome lay in the hands of the gods, Stuart was occupied for the best part of an hour. When he came back to the auditorium, he opened the door of the projection box door. George grinned and gave the thumbs up sign. So far Willie was still there. Stuart stood at the back of the stalls and waited. The film was nearing the end: Lulu, destitute by now in London, left by her two companions to try and make some money, picks up a client, who is going to turn out to be Jack the Ripper. She takes him to her flat. He is a tormented character, but is at first in awe of Lulu's almost ethereal presence in candlelight. The film cuts to one of her companions tucking into a meal; the other, unaware of the danger she faces, joins a Salvation Army procession, led by its band.

Stuart strained his eyes, trying to gauge Willie's body language. He certainly wasn't asleep. He was intent, bent slightly forward from the support of the seatback. But Stuart was too far away to be sure; he walked on tiptoe down the aisle and sat in the same row on the opposite side. Willie didn't see him. He was completely absorbed.

The film ended. Willie sat there. George brought up the dimmed lights to a brighter level. Willie didn't stir. Stuart stood up and crossed to the row in front of Willie and sat on the armrest and faced him. Willie looked at him, as though he'd been wakened out of a trance. Then he focused his eyes intently on Stuart.

'It's not right. No, it's not right. The girl didn't deserve that. It wasn't her fault. What upbringing did she have?' Willie said spontaneously.

Stuart nodded in sympathy, but he was amazed at Willie's sensitive response.

'The actress plays her part very well. What do you think of her?' he cautiously ventured.

Willie opened his hands, as though in appeal, 'Her delicate face, her hair bob and the look in her eyes.' Willie's face was animated as he spoke. 'Her eyes can express such sadness. She was like. . . she was a porcelain figure come to life.'

Stuart smiled. This was the man who handled delicate artefacts in his shop, a man who spent years among finely painted pottery and glassware.

'In three weeks we'll have another film by the same director and with the same star; it's called *Diary of a Lost Girl*. I think you would like it too.'

Immediately, Willie nodded vigorously, 'Yes, I would like to see it.'

'You could come to the first house, after you shut up the shop. Sit in the balcony. It has tiered seating. No one in a hat's going to spoil your view.'

Willie put his hand up to his waistcoat pocket and took out a small diary, 'What day is it on?'

'Wednesday and Thursday.'

'I'll come on the Wednesday.'

'And next week, there's a British film called *Blackmail*. It's Alfred Hitchcock's first talking picture. I think it would interest you.'

'You think so? When will you be showing it?'

'Monday and Tuesday.'

Willie noted the days in his diary, and put it in his pocket. He stood up. 'Thank you,' he said. They walked towards the exit.

According to law, alcohol was not served in licensed hotels on Sundays in Scotland, except to bona fide travellers, so Helen didn't expect the Royal Hotel to be very busy. She'd taken longer than usual in getting ready to go out; and now she stood by the mirror in the hall with her mother scrutinizing her final preparations. She chose her best silk scarf; it set off the navy blue coat. The weather was dry and held the promise of remaining so. Finally satisfied, and with her mother's approving nod, she set off.

A few minutes after the clock in the Tolbooth tower struck three, slightly nervous, she arrived at the hotel steps. Stuart was waiting inside. He greeted her with a warm smile, and took her coat and hung it by his on the stand. He showed the way into the dining room.

There were about eight or nine others in the room; and Helen knew most of them: middle-aged couples, two well-dressed ladies and two or three elderly men at the rear of the room. For certain, her being here with Stuart Robertson would be all over the town tomorrow because two well-known Clashbags were having afternoon tea. Stuart, taking in at a quick glance all who were in the room, turned his back to them. 'Will we sit there by the window?' he asked, pointing to a table for two overlooking the High Street.

'Yes, that would do fine.' Then Helen went on, 'I've not been here, in this dining room before.'

'I've lunches here during the week. If they're very busy I get a place in the hotel's kitchen.'

She laughed, 'It must be an unusual life, eating out every day and working late into the evening?'

'You get used to it.'

A young waitress in a black dress with a white pinny took their order.

At work she was used to the two men in the partnership leading when it came to social chit-chat, and so she was content at the start to let him do the talking. He asked about the Girl Guide movement: how long she'd been involved in it; where they usually went to on annual summer camp; and how thriving the company was. The waitress brought a tray of scones, cakes and shortbread. Helen poured from the teapot.

'Do you expect to be left here long, or will they move you around?' Helen asked, taking the initiative, and changing the topic.

'Perhaps three years, and then I think they'll move me to somewhere bigger.'

'What made you choose the world of cinema for a career?'

'I was fascinated that film, still photographs linked together, could be made into an art really. I discovered it when I was a boy and was given a magic lantern one summer holiday.'

'The pictures are a new world to me.'

'Now you've seen a "talkie" do you think you might want to see others?'

'Yes, *Anna Christie* was a good story; you were drawn in to it. At times though, it was a bit like a stage play.'

'It was adapted from a play, and it shows at times. Some reviewers have scoffed at the way Greta Garbo asks for whisky and ginger, and her "don't be stingy, baby."'

'But I preferred it to the silent film.'

'I think as they improve the sound equipment, they'll be more realistic.'

Then, he came out with the unexpected, 'I saw you from the gallery at the Remembrance service. You were very sombre. Was it someone especially dear to you?'

She was taken unaware, and nodded, 'Yes, it was.' There was a silence, neither spoke. Then Helen said, 'We'd been going together since we were at school.'

Stuart nodded, but didn't comment.

Then Helen recovered her composure, and asked him how he found his accommodation, and they chatted lightly and easily. They talked about life in small towns, and Helen relaxed again and was soon animated. He had just asked her what she'd been reading recently.

'They do a lovely afternoon tea don't they Helen?' The speaker interrupting them was Linda Graham, her gimlet eye at odds with the friendly greeting. She had been with one of her golfing partners, Louise Smith. Helen registered their presence further back in the room when she came in; but, now, on the point of leaving, and about to reach the door, Linda, after a word with her friend, crossed over to their table with a very purposeful step. Then she turned to Stuart, 'But isn't it sinful, those little indulgences we allow ourselves?'

Stuart smiled weakly, and looked slightly uncomfortable for the moment, not the assured manager of the cinema.

'Yes. We should know better though,' he said.

Linda smiled in return; rather forced Helen thought. And then, saying her farewell, Linda departed. Helen and Stuart took up from where they left off. When at last they rose to leave, to Helen's surprise, the afternoon had passed quickly.

He offered to walk her home, but she told him she was going round to visit her friend Joyce. That was a clear signal for him; and they parted at the hotel steps. They had just got to know one another. No commitments to meeting again; but he offered to hand a card into her office when the next film he thought she might like was coming up.

The air was unusually mild, almost delicate for so late in the year. The stars were all obscured. The street lamps diffused a soft amber glow, and lighted windowpanes framed the quiet streets. She felt acutely attuned to the scene she was walking through, as though it had been arranged for her in an empty theatre by an unseen stage-manager.

She went over the afternoon again as she walked. She'd warmed to him as before. He was relaxed and smiled with his eyes. She thought about how he conducted himself. He didn't play a macho role and dominate the conversation. He seemed to leave it to her, she thought, to make up her mind. He was certainly interested in her.

But their being together would come up in the office tomorrow. Be prepared for it. The Clash would embellish it in their fashion, and Linda would spread it on the fairways. Well, she didn't need to talk; she had a reputation.

All of a sudden, a gut-wrenching, disagreeable thought struck Helen. Surely not! But the idea persisted. That forceful greeting in the hotel began to take on another meaning. Gloating. Bitchy. What an end to the afternoon! She straightened her back. Well I can play at that game too.

And next day was a good time to do it. Around 4pm Helen rang Linda's front doorbell. She had taken a devious route on her way to deliver a missive to a household, telling her boss she had some Girl Guide errand to see to at the same time.

'What a nice surprise Helen,' Linda said. 'Come in.'

'No thank you Linda, it'll not take a moment. I've to get back to the office. There wasn't time yesterday. I was wondering if you would be prepared to be a tester for one of the guide proficiency badges?'

'Ah, I see.' Linda said. Her face muscles relaxed.

'It's the Hostess badge,' Helen went on. 'There's no one I can think of who would be more suitable than yourself to be our tester.'

'That's kind of you,' Linda said, with only a trace of being ruffled. 'My problem is that I'm on the Golf Club Committee and it takes up a lot of my free time. So I really couldn't take on another commitment.'

'That's a shame. I wanted to ask you before we send out the Newsletter to parents tomorrow. I would have included your appointment if you had been willing,' Helen said, with a resigned shake of the head.

On her way back to the office, a reaction set in, and the full extent of the risk she'd taken hit her. If Linda had accepted, there would have been parental repercussions; her own judgment as a guide leader would have been questioned.

The Clash concentrated on the cinema, centre of a sinister spider's web.

'A cosy three-some they had of it in the hotel in the afternoon.'

'It's maybe the same at night.'

'The cinema's a corrupting influence.'

'Company directors need to know.'

'That manager should be in the jail.'

At a cursory glance from the commercial traveller, fortifying himself with a cup of coffee before taking his wares to a shop owner, the trio at a Formica-topped table at the rear of the café could have been local businessmen mulling over some project. But Stuart Robertson, John Cameron, wearing collar and tie, and Willie Meikle were discussing Alfred Hitchcock's first talking picture, *Blackmail*.

John had gone to the cinema the previous week, as they'd agreed, to find out how Willie had reacted to watching a film.

'Your friend short-arse responded sensitively to *Pandora's Box*. He wasn't slavering at the mouth nor was he at all outraged. A strong moral sense of injustice, I think. He's coming back for more,' Stuart said.

'The age of miracles has not passed.'

Stuart told him about the films he had recommended to Willie, and John decided to go and see *Blackmail* on the evening that Willie would be there. After the film, Stuart took John aside in the foyer as the audience left, and they waited until Willie appeared among the file coming down the balcony stairs. In the brief discussion, Stuart asked Willie if he could take half an hour away from his shop next morning and they would talk about the film. Willie agreed.

John could not but marvel at the turn of events, as they sat round the café table.

'What did you think of the girl character? Was she right to run from the scene of the killing?' Stuart asked Willie.

'She wasn't to blame. She had to defend herself,' Willie said.

'Well the character was called Alice, and that was the name of my wife, so I couldn't but be sympathetic towards her,' John chipped in. But he quickly went on, 'The film raises some interesting moral questions. Was her boyfriend policeman, Frank, right in pocketing the evidence of her glove. Should love for his girl come before justice?'

'Aye, that's a hard one,' Willie said.

'Shouldn't she just have gone to the police at once, and explained that it was self-defence?' Stuart asked, looking at Willie, keen to draw him out further.

'Would they have believed her? Very handy for them that. She tells them where the body is, and says that she did it. Solves a problem for them. They would make her pay for it.'

'That director likes to pose questions for the audience. He seems interested in asking about right and wrong,' Stuart said.

'Well there you have it,' Willie said. 'The policeman pockets the glove. He knows what they're like when they've an easy target, he's one of them.'

John was still coming to terms with the bane of his life in the kirk session talking earnestly about a film, and it took him a while to get into his stride. 'Good point.'

'The director, Alfred Hitchcock, makes an appearance in the film. Remember the scene in the train where a chubby man is sitting reading and a cheeky wee boy flattens his hat? That's Hitchcock,' Stuart said.

'He doesn't care that he's being laughed at?' Willie said.

'Seemingly not.'

'How did they get that filming done in the British Museum at the end when the blackmailer falls through the glass dome?' John asked.

'Ah, that bit was trick filming, they call the Shuftan process, where they use a mirror at an angle to the camera,' Stuart said, 'and they reflect a picture of the real place in it.'

'What did you make of the recurring shots of the painting of the laughing jester that was in the victim's flat?' John said, 'The last shot of the film is the ripped painting laughing at us.'

'If the director fellow has that kind of sense of humour, maybe he's laughing at us,' Willie said.

They talked on for a good half hour.

Helen didn't jump at Stuart's first film recommendation. But she read a review of his next suggestion, *The Divorcee*; this time a reluctant Joyce came along with her to the second night.

'I don't want to be a gooseberry.'

'You won't. I'll be lucky if he gives me two minutes of his precious time.'

'Girls at work were saying it's about people having affairs and marriages breaking up.'

'The review in the paper said it's very good. The director is a Robert Leonard. Seems he was recommended for an Academy Award for Best Director, but didn't win it. And Norma Shearer got the Award for Best Actress.'

Stuart wasn't in sight when they went up to the cashier's box. They took seats in the stalls; and they settled down with a tube of Rowntree's Fruit Pastilles.

At the end of the show, people were coming out into the foyer by both doors from the stalls. Stuart was on duty as they appeared. He stepped forward.

'I saw you going in from the projection box.'

'Stuart, this is my friend Joyce,' Helen said.

They shook hands.

'Did you like it?' Stuart asked, including both of them in the question. He didn't try to steer them towards the outside landing.

'I did, I really did,' Helen said emphatically. 'A film about weak men. It was true to life.'

Stuart smiled; Joyce looked on with interest, knowing her friend had the bit between her teeth, and wouldn't stop until she got there; wherever there was.

'And it was also about double standards of morality for men and women,' Helen said.

'Tell me more about that.'

'The Paul character feels sorry for himself when Norma Shearer chooses someone else; he gets drunk, causes an accident and the girl in the car with him, Dorothy, ends up disfigured, and he marries her out of pity. Then when Norma Shearer's husband has an affair, he tells her it was nothing at all. But when she is on her own and lonely and has an affair, he leaves her. One standard for men, another for women.'

Stuart stood, smiling and nodding; then he raised his eyebrows at Joyce, as Helen sallied on, waxing eloquent. Joyce grinned.

'The only worthy character,' continued Helen, 'was Norma Shearer's: she didn't want to cause another divorce when Tom was prepared to leave Dorothy and marry her.'

'True enough,' Stuart smiled and nodded. 'Did you like Norma Shearer's performance?'

'Yes, very convincing.'

'Did you enjoy it Joyce?'

'Yes, I liked it, I thought it was very good.'

There were fewer people in the foyer now, but the doorman was standing at the top of the steps, anticipating the signal to let the queue move.

'Do you never have any time off?' Helen asked, in the condescending tone of a superior patron.

'I will when our trainee starts in January,' he laughed.

'We'll need to go,' Helen said. She and Joyce joined the tail of customers retreating down the flight of steps.

Midnight's chimes on the study clock startled John Cameron out of reverie. He read over the letter he'd written once more, and then he signed it. A copy of the *Glasgow Herald* lay open at the job vacancy page on his desk.

He couldn't go back to where he had been up until three weeks ago. *All Quiet on the Western Front* had been a watershed for him. It had exposed him to his own intellectual dishonesty. He had to come to terms with his loss of faith. He couldn't stay in the trough of mindlessness he'd been in for ten years. He had long discussions in his mind with Alice about it. And he went to the cinema. Films took him away from his own thoughts. He didn't wear his clerical collar, he wore corduroy trousers and a fisherman's jersey under his old army greatcoat, he had had dyed black.

But as far as his parish work went, he was distracted. He was late in fulfilling his schedule of parish visits. It was December, and he had got behind. He carried out those visits twice a year, in the spring and autumn. And among those on his list he had still to see was Linda Graham. He'd heard rumours about her. Sometimes, droplets from the potent brew of the Clash filtered through to him. When that happened (usually via an office-bearer in the church, who discovered that the minister wasn't shocked if tittle-tattle was repeated in his hearing) John made no comment.

But hearsay was partly confirmed for him, on his last visit, one afternoon in April, when, he was pretty sure, the widow had given him the come-hither. He parried, playing the innocent, letting it go over his head.

Now she was on his list for the week. He'd been delayed for a long time at the house of a non-church-goer who was very ill and in need of reassurance that his life had amounted to something worthwhile. By the time John called on Linda Graham, it was getting dark. Linda welcomed him. She looked elegant. Her dark hair was held back in a clasp, and had a prominent streak of grey along the left side. A slim silver chain stood out against her dark cashmere top; she had a full figure, and the flared skirt suited her. She showed him into her tastefully furnished sitting-room. There was a three-piece suite in a floral design of faded roses scattered among healthy leaves; a large, patterned wool rug was spread on the floor in front of the coal fire. She offered him the left hand side of the three-seater sofa, and she sat on its far side. She was quite animated to begin with, talking about golf and her sense of finding peace on the golf course. He had no interest in golf and just nodded politely.

Linda became quiet for a moment. Then, in completely relaxed fashion, she raised her left heel on to her right knee; the flared skirt allowed her to clasp her raised left knee with both hands; and the action had the effect of unconsciously drawing his attention to her thigh although it was covered. She turned her face towards him with wide-eyed demure appeal, her elegantly adorned neck held in tension, her lips slightly parted. Suddenly, it registered with him: it was the pose adopted by Marlene Dietrich playing Lola-Lola in the night club scene in Josef von Sternberg's *The Blue Angel*. The film, he had seen last week, was a masterly evocation of a morality tale — the temptress who lured the respectable professor on to the shoals of humiliation. Linda must have seen the poster, or she'd gone to the film.

All at once, she sighed, and, releasing her raised knee, she stretched out her left hand and placed it on the back of his hand on the sofa. 'A person needs the human touch,' and she looked intently into his eyes; she slipped her hand round his and held it. Then she moved along the sofa in one easy glide, and sat closer to him, all the while holding his hand. He made no attempt to take it back.

Suddenly, everything made sense to him: they both needed physical comfort. He leaned closer, put his hand behind her head, held the nape of her neck and looked into her eyes. She smiled and brought her lips to his.

They didn't move out of the warm sitting-room. They lay on the luxurious wool rug. He was amazed — after all those years of abstinence. And he silenced the refrains of guilt the instant they sounded; and he gave himself up to the moment.

When they finally got up off the floor and composed themselves, Linda sat back in an armchair and he on the sofa. They were quiet for a few moments, looking at each other fondly.

'Would you like a cup of tea?' she asked.

'Yes, that would be nice.'

She got up at once and went into the kitchen.

He felt as though he'd undergone a chemical change and emerged a new compound. He stretched back on the sofa, suffused in a warm after-glow; and he thought about Linda's attitude to life. She probably had a simple faith that wasn't at odds with her need of comfort through human contact. She had created her own philosophy for living; you had to admire her for it.

Walking back to the manse an hour later, he didn't agonize over his misdemeanour. The flesh is weak, that's all. It was no more serious than that. But he wouldn't go back. Even one more trip before the spring and the Clash would have the scandal through the town. They might even already have spread it: he was coming back from a visit so late in the day.

But he didn't feel that he'd betrayed his love for Alice. And, at that moment, Heloise and Abelard came to his mind, the pair that symbolized lasting love. He'd visited their tomb at the cemetery of *Père Lachaise* in Paris when he had a leave during the war.

He was surprised how calm he felt.

Helen and Joyce weren't both free on the same night when *Diary of a Lost Girl* was playing, so Helen went on her own. Stuart's note told her that this director, Georg Pabst, had great sensitivity for the way young women were often treated in society; and he assured her she would like the star, Louise Brooks.

Right from the start, Helen responded to the pacing of the silent film. The intertitles didn't crop up often and you had the time to add your own thoughts to the actions as they were happening on the screen.

The film was set in German society; some of its scenes seared Helen. The unfairness of the way the Louise Brooks character, Thymian Henning, was treated; the cruelty of people and systems roused Helen's feelings; and the sadness of the human lot overshadowed all. Working in a lawyer's office had made her sensitive to the miseries that people endure at the hands of their fellows. Fragments from letters that crossed her desk, pleading unjust treatment at the hands of a more powerful person went through her mind. But then, at the scene in the film that takes place in a lawyer's office, the image that flashed in her mind was of the hulking farmer she had rejected two years ago — the submissive retreat; his bent back as he left the office, rejected and humiliated. She felt a stab of remorse in the darkened theatre; she could have refused him more sensitively. Thymian Henning was feisty, and fought back. Some people didn't.

In the front row of the balcony, Willie Meikle sat, completely absorbed. He lived in the story, and reacted fiercely to the scenes of the institution to which Louise Brooks had been shamefully committed. His blood pressure was fired up; during some scenes, he held the overhanging lip of the balcony ledge in both hands.

At the end of the film he remained in his seat until those behind had exited.

Helen came into the foyer on her way out, and made straight towards Stuart.

'It was a lovely film,' she said. And she screwed up her eyes, 'So sad. And those last words that came up on the screen, "A little more love, and no one would be lost in this world."' She tightened her eyes together.

Stuart took her by the elbow and stepped back, guiding her with him so that she wasn't facing people leaving the cinema.

'Yes, it's a touching film,' he said, instinctively guessing that he had to take her focus away from herself. But she was locked into her thoughts.

'People can be lost and not know it,' Helen said. Tears were coming. 'I have to go.' She felt she might cry in front of people. She turned quickly, stepped out on the landing, pulled her coat tightly around her, and ran lightly down the steps.

He was watching her cross Tower Street to the pavement on the other side, when, out of the corner of his eye, he saw Willie Meikle coming down the balcony stairs. Willie had his coat slung over his arm.

Stuart continued looking at the retreating figure of Helen. Then he turned back to the customers; Willie had found a space in front of the cashier's box, and he was struggling into his overcoat, with his back towards the dwindling numbers leaving.

Stuart stepped forward and helped him, lifting the collar up to his shoulders. Surprised at the ease with which the last movement was accomplished, Willie automatically turned round. His eyes were red-rimmed. He looked at Stuart, and shook his head slightly, and tried a weak smile. But he couldn't speak. He would have been overcome if he'd tried. Stuart smiled and placed a friendly hand on Willie's shoulder.

Willie, a diminutive figure in his overcoat, stood a moment or two on the landing, carrying with him images and meaning from the film that he didn't want to put into words. He pulled his cloth cap out of his pocket, adjusted it on his head, and, holding on to the rail, slowly descended the steps into the December night.

As Helen walked home, the film weighed on her. She felt physically weak, as though she was recovering from an illness. 'A little more love and no one would be lost in this world.' Until this evening, she had never for a moment thought that she might be lost. She had lived with a shade for years; she had deliberately avoided emotional involvement. She might be no different from her boss, Archie MacNair. Perhaps she had lost the capacity to love?

Her mother knew immediately that she was upset. But Helen only said that it was a sad film.

A few hours later a bank of cloud shredded slowly and unveiled a silver bark in full sail above the Sutherland hills. A path of moonlight stretched from it across the water of the Dornoch Firth, from the north to the south shore, inviting him to the galley where the boatman would set a course and take them over the sea to *Tir nan Òg*. Willie stood at his window overlooking the firth. He gazed in wonder. It drew his spirit outwards. He thought of the film he'd seen; of the final words on the screen; and he thought of his own life.

But he was very cold. He couldn't get warm. His body was chilled. He left the curtains open on the scene, and went into the kitchen and fixed himself a second hot-water bottle.

Moonlight stole into his room. He was so cold. He lay in bed with his eyes open. Mentally he projected scenes from the film on to the beam of moonlight playing on the wall opposite the window.

Gradually, he began to doze and at last fell into sleep. Then, after a while, a steel vice gripped his chest, and its torque tightened and tightened; until he no longer felt cold.

A section of veteran Clashbags said that it was self-inflicted. Willie had seen a film of such depravity it undermined his faith and his will to live, and he drank a full bottle of whisky. With his small frame, that did for him!

But another cadre of equally seasoned Clashbags had it that he was TT but had a bad heart, like his father before him who died young. He came from poor stock. What could you expect?

'Could we have a word afterwards?' the Rev Henry Crawford, presbytery clerk, said softly, leaning forward towards him, as John Cameron, was about to convene the sub-committee.

After the others had left and the vestry door was closed, Henry Crawford showed signs of being agitated: his eyes blinked quickly, and he licked his bottom lip. He was well-fleshed, in his early sixties, and had committee business in his very bones. He had announced when he arrived that he was there *ex officio*, in his capacity as presbytery clerk, lingering on his enunciation of the Latin.

'It's a delicate matter. Rumour has reached me at Presbytery that, that . . .' He grimaced and began afresh, 'It's been alleged that there may have been impropriety on your part in the course of a parish visit. With a certain lady,' he added as a hurried afterthought.

John Cameron got the drift at once of where this was going; he wasn't going to make it any easier for the busybody, and a smile creased his face, 'Go on. You were saying it was a certain lady.'

'Well, yes. A lady, who, it seems, has a reputation.'

'And what kind of reputation Henry?'

'John, you're bound to know. A promiscuous reputation.' Beads of sweat stood out on his forehead, although the gas fire was at a low setting and the vestry was far from warm. 'We don't want a breath of scandal in the parish.'

'So I take it that, to mix metaphors, you're wondering if I've been getting my oats on a pastoral visit,' John said, grinning openly now.

Henry Crawford gave way to a gasp of exasperation, 'I know you chaps who were in the trenches can have difficulties that last for years. Difficulties, well, that can cause erratic behaviour. But look here man, we are responsible for our actions.'

John leaned across the table towards his interlocutor, 'Speaking of trenches, and personal responsibilities, I was reading recently that in the heady days of late 1914, you were urging young men to arms, to fight the good fight. Only you were incautious enough to do it in the newspapers, proclaiming that; what were your words again? "that the road might be bloody, but the rewards would be great," if I remember rightly.'

Henry flushed in anger, but before he could get a word out, John continued.

'Before the Remembrance service, I checked on the 1911 Census figures for the burgh, and set the number of its war dead against it. You might be surprised to learn that the town sacrificed 1 in 13 of its total adult population. The 1/4thSeaforths, the Ross-shire battalion, lost 28.8% of those who served. All of that seems bloody enough to me. Do you feel any share of responsibility?'

'I'll not be judged by you Cameron.'

'Nor I by you Crawford. I would hope that we're both judged at a higher level.'

The presbytery clerk made as though to move back his chair from the table, 'I've come to you as a brother in Christ.'

'To do what exactly?'

'To desist from visiting the lady in question. I could arrange a locum to carry out some of your parish visits.'

'And you've come with that proposal as a brother in Christ. Is that the same Christ who was friend of publicans and sinners? And didn't we learn in New Testament Studies that Mary Magdalene was perhaps a former prostitute?'

Having completely lost the initiative he held at first, his anger sparked, the presbytery clerk moved his chair back.

'Listen carefully,' John went on, 'I'll carry on doing all my duties on my own. Until, that is, the Presbytery decide otherwise, and they'll need more than a Clashbag tale to do that.'

The presbytery clerk was on his feet.

'But I've something to say that'll be music to your ears,' John said. 'I've applied for a teaching post in higher education.'

Henry Crawford, paused as he was about to pick up his coat from the back of a chair, and stood, stock-still.

'Could I put you down for an additional reference?' John asked, in mock supplicatory tone.

'You assuredly could,' said the presbytery clerk, putting on his coat, 'Good night.'

John Cameron sat at the table a little longer, looking at the closed varnished door. Then he turned off the gas fire.

Winter gripped the town, and shook it in its claws. Flurries of snow fell; then showers of freezing rain followed. Overhead wires collapsed under the weight of ice. In the middle of January, north-east gales battered the land, and the national grid line from the south came down. After two days, power was restored, but then as life returned to normal, heavy snow fell continuously for twelve hours. The process of digging out left hard-packed snow on the streets. So long as there was electric power though, the cinema attracted fair sized audiences.

Helen's mother needed no persuading to come with her daughter and Joyce into the snowy streets one evening to see the musical, *The Love Parade*.

'It was like a fairy tale setting,' her mother said afterwards. The three were arm in arm for mutual support on the deserted roadway. It was easier walking on the hard-packed snow on the road than on the pavements. 'Who was the girl playing the queen of Sylvania?'

'Jeanette MacDonald. She had a lovely voice,' Helen said.

'The music alone lifts you out of this grim weather,' Joyce said.

'I don't know how she felt like singing in her nightie in front of all those ladies in waiting,' Mrs Ross laughed.

'There were some gorgeous dresses,' Joyce said.

They talked about the film until it came to the parting of the ways, where Joyce left them and cut off on another street that took her home.

'He is a nice fellow, that manager. Courteous, and he has a pleasant manner. It was good of him to have three seats reserved for us.'

'Yes, he's quite nice.' Helen could tell that her mother had taken a shine to him.

'What was the problem did he say he was having?'

'The film they were supposed to be having next is going to be unavailable. His head office wanted to give a substitute and he wanted something else. He had to be on the phone to them every half hour,' Helen said.

'If you can, come and see *Borderline* next week, on Monday,' Stuart had said to John Cameron. 'I've limited scope for programming. I've managed to get one or two. But top brass at head office think this film will only do even half well in a big centre where there's a student population. They've reluctantly agreed on the condition it's for one night only. In case it flops. But I'm hoping it won't flop. It's directed by Kenneth Macpherson, and stars the African-American singer Paul Robeson. You'll find it interesting.'

John said he would be there.

A thaw got underway over the week-end and movement on the streets became easier.

There was no time to discuss the film at the end of the first house on Monday: Stuart was there in the foyer, asking customers what they thought of the film; and their trainee, Andrew Douglas, stood on the outside landing, doing the same with the younger age group. They seemed to have split the work between them to get the opinion of as many as possible. Stuart briefly asked John if they could meet in the café next morning.

'I wasn't sure what to make of some of it. Striking images. It doesn't hold back from dealing with prejudice against race,' John said, as they sat in the café.

'There's a lot to be said for it.'

'The fact it's set in a town, not a big city, made the point about racial prejudice even stronger. It could happen here.'

'Some reviewers have damned it,' Stuart said. 'But they aren't always right. The public can respond and understand a film. We got a good response from customers. They could relate to the prejudice that forces Paul Robeson to leave town.'

'The director went in for shots that stay on people and objects. He seems to want images to carry meaning.'

'He does that in post-production editing.'

'Where was it filmed do you know?'

'Switzerland. That's where he's based.'

'Switzerland! That reminds me, did you read that *All Quiet on the Western Front* has been banned in Germany?'

'I did. A group of Nazis rioted in Berlin. Forced the government's hand.'

'Maybe the next step is for governments to use film for their own purposes?'

Stuart's plan to spread the management load and extend the number of screenings was not going to happen in the timescale he wanted. He discussed it with George Anderson. They agreed about the problem: Andrew Douglas.

'I want to speak to you. Close the door.' There was a hard edge to Stuart Robertson's voice, as he swung round in his swivel chair to face Andrew. Andrew stood there, suddenly uncertain.

'What do you think you're playing at? For the first month you were interested in what you were doing. Now, you're going about your work like a half-shut knife. I'm not going to carry a passenger.'

Andrew went pale. He stood, silent.

'What's got into you? Is there a problem at home? Have you stopped revising for your exams? Is it girl trouble?'

Andrew shook his head.

'Well, what is it then?'

'It's . . . it's just the same, the same every day,' Andrew blurted out, 'just rewind reels; switch on projector B when I get the signal; keep an inventory of the carbon arc lamps. It's not . . .'

'Interesting. Or challenging enough. Is that what you mean?'

Andrew nodded.

'If you were on your own tonight, could you switch projectors on cue for a feature?'

'Yes.'

'Can you splice a broken print?'

'Yes.'

'You're able to do what you're supposed to do in the time you've been here. And you'll keep doing that for a couple of months more until you can thread a projector with your eyes shut. Now, if you can't cope with that . . .'

Andrew's bottom lip quivered slightly, 'You're right. I was disappointed. I think that's what's wrong.'

'It's natural to be disappointed,' the manager said in a kinder tone. 'But you'll get over that. You've got to master these tasks before you're ready to get more responsibility. The question is can you live with that?'

'Yes, yes I can. I'm sorry.'

'I know what it's like at first,' the manager said, gesturing with an open hand, 'But you'll get through it,' he said, nodding encouragingly. 'All right?'

'Yes.'

'Good. If you put your back into it, we'll begin children's matinees on Saturday mornings. You'll be in the projection box on your own. Could you cope?'

'Yes, definitely.'

'Back to work then.'

Half an hour later, Stuart was talking with the cashier in the foyer when George Anderson appeared. Stuart gestured with his head towards his office.

'How did it go?' George asked, but there was a smile playing on his lips.

'I put the frighteners on him. He got the message. I think he'll be all right.'

In as much as there was a eureka moment John could point to in later years and say to himself that was when he resolved the tension he he'd been living with since he had seen the war film, it was on that sunny February morning he walked in the manse grounds to view the snow-covered hills across the blue expanse of firth. There were still snowdrifts along the roadsides, and pockets of it slowly melting in the manse grounds. That was when he found a wreath of snow about eight inches high, melted into the shape of an arc, and held within its points, facing south, a clump of snowdrops. They had endured the most savage winter in years to reveal their delicate beauty. Alice would have loved them. She would have found these before he did. When they were students, they used to walk in Glasgow's Kelvin Grove to look for the first snowdrops.

Of course, flashes of insight had been coalescing for him over the winter months. Going to the cinema and reading late into the night had helped. But it wasn't a smooth incline to a solution: there were peaks and troughs. He had had hours of inner peace after his visit to Linda Graham; that afternoon had a lasting impact. He found a lesson there; and he appreciated its irony: a man of God coming to terms with a spiritual dilemma thanks to an afternoon with someone whom the devout would call a scarlet woman.

And of the future: if he got the job he'd applied for, fine; if he didn't, so be it. He would take one step at a time. No voice would speak to him out of the clouds, pointing the way forward for him. And he had come to see that it would always be like this for him: what he had to do was to endure. And the nodding snowdrop heads agreed.

Spring came with a rush. In the soft evening light the fields were awakening from their winter sleep; they had been ploughed, and the open furrows gave out a breath that hung low in the air. High to the west, pink-tinged banks of cloud drifted eastwards.

Helen chose a five-mile circular route around Rosemount. At first she and Stuart talked about the changing face of the countryside and the best walks at this time of year. After about two miles, they stopped by the bridge over the Aldie burn. The water ran clear, gurgling, eager to join a larger confluence. A few birch trees grew by the bridge. Although their catkins had formed, they were still faintly lime-green; and they swayed and dipped in the faint breath of the west wind.

Helen was wearing a Fair Isle cardigan that her mother had knitted, a tweed skirt and stout walking shoes. She looked down at the water for a bit, then, leaning against the stonework, she asked, 'Were you a pacifist on religious grounds?'

'No, I didn't believe in God. I felt the war was about national status and power. We were being manipulated by politicians.'

She nodded, then stretched out over the stone parapet and cupped her palm round a catkin. It hung delicate and pendulous against her palm, 'I never knew anyone who was a pacifist.'

'If you had, would you have despised him?'

She flushed a little, 'No, people should be entitled to their beliefs.' And she paused, looking down at the fast-flowing burn, 'Sometimes, thoughts like that might have come in. You can have conflicting thoughts. But I wouldn't have been proud of myself.'

Afterwards, it seemed to her that he had known intuitively how to set the moment to ask her about Alan. She'd released the catkin, and pushed with her palms against the bridge, and looked at Stuart, as though signalling they continue walking, when he stepped in front of her, took hold of her under the arms, swiftly straightened his knees and lifted her on to the parapet of the bridge.

She squealed, and then laughed. She hadn't been frolicked with for years.

'It must have been hard for you when you lost your fiancé,' Stuart said right out of the blue.

Surprised, she placed her palms on the parapet, as if to jump down. But he moved in and lifted her off the bridge. She sighed, looked down at the road,

'Yes,' she said. Then she raised her eyes and looked into his. 'It was. It would have been worse if I hadn't had my mother. She could understand, and I could talk to her.'

'But it must have taken a long time to get over it,' Stuart said.

'Oh yes,' she gave a sigh. 'I kept the flame alive. Maybe. Oh maybe . . . Let's leave it.'

'Is that what you meant,' Stuart persisted, 'the night we showed *Diary of a Lost Girl* that one might be lost and not know it? Lost in the past?'

'I think I dwelt on what once was too much,' Helen said.

Stuart held out his left hand, touched her elbow, 'And we have to live in the present.' He gestured in the direction they had been walking, and said, 'Will we carry on?'

They began walking again, and they were both silent for a short while. Then Helen changed the subject back to him. 'You said you didn't believe in God, but you went to church for the Remembrance service.'

'You can change with the years. I wouldn't call myself an out-and-out atheist now. I don't hold with the idea of a God with the carrot and the stick of an afterlife. But I think there's maybe a creative mover behind it all; behind the universe.'

Some large Scots pine trees overhung the road at one point. A carpet of pine needles lay before them; and they walked through them. Stuart stooped and picked up a fallen pine cone. 'It's perfect,' he said as he handed it to her. 'The pine cone was an important symbol to the ancients. It represented fertility and long life.'

87

Helen took it and smiled in return. They resumed their walk, but Stuart saw that tears had come to her eyes. She said nothing, but held the cone in her hand for the rest of the walk.

They stood a moment or two by Helen's gate. It was as if a formal pattern was being observed, and each knew the code. There was no touching, no good-bye kiss. Helen said, 'I enjoyed that walk.'

'So did I.'

'It's often nice in the evening at this time of year,' Helen said.

'What about Sunday evening, if it's fine?'

'Would you like to come here, and meet my mother properly?'

Stuart smiled, 'Yes,' he said.

Helen's mother was a little under medium height for a woman, and her hair had turned prematurely grey. She had delicate features and a quickness of spirit. Stuart took to her right away. And she played her part well: she was neither effusive nor distant with him. Before he met her, he had wondered if she might have become the sort of possessive mother who wanted to keep her unmarried daughter at home with her, to be a help to her in her very old age. But he didn't sense that position at all.

Helen went into the kitchen and left Stuart and her mother to talk. It was still cool in the April evenings, and a low fire burned in the hearth. He could hear the sound of a kettle boiling, and cups and saucers being placed on a tray.

'Helen will have told you she had a young man who was killed in the war?'

'Yes, she told me.'

'Be patient. She was very young when the lad was killed. She took a long time to get over it, and find a life for herself. She's a strong girl. Be patient with her.'

He smiled, 'Yes, it's all right.' He felt touched by her trust, telling him this.

Helen reappeared with tea and shortbread. She was relaxed and her mother was at ease. Stuart didn't stay too late; and, reflecting on it as he walked back to his lodging, he thought the evening had gone well.

After they had tidied up the kitchen in preparation for the weekday routine that lay ahead, Helen went up to her room. She didn't draw the curtains, but let the gloaming light her bedroom. And she took out an old shoebox from the foot of the wardrobe. It contained a bundle of letters in their buff-coloured official paper, tied with a ribbon. She sat on her bed with the bundle in her lap. She toyed with the ribbon but didn't undo the knot. She sat, instead, looking out at the changing cloud formation until the twilight faded. Then with her index finger and thumb, she flicked the bow of the ribbon, replaced the bundle in the box, and put it back at the bottom of the wardrobe. Then she closed the curtains.

Stuart's departure came sooner than expected.

'It's Mr Ritchie for you,' said the clerk in that serious tone reserved for when senior company officials came on the phone.

'Hello Bill.'

'Morning Stuart. Two things: your programming initiatives, showing art house films, have worked well. We're taking up the idea with one or two other of our outlets. So well done.'

'Thanks Bill.'

'The not so good news is that we've had another letter complaining about your moral turpitude. Are you running Roman orgies in the cinema?'

'What?' said Stuart, incredulous. 'What are you saying?'

'It's anonymous, of course, these things always are. And it's destined for the waste paper basket.' They both lapsed into silence for a moment, Stuart to take in the information, and Bill Ritchie, to measure out the remains of his news. 'You haven't taken up with someone's wife have you? You've certainly made an enemy.'

'Bill you know quite well you get malicious gossip. You always get some nut-case who's jealous of success or something.'

'I know. But this is the third of them we've received, so there's a pattern; they're typewritten, and there's tenacity there. I didn't mention the others over the past few months, but this is what I'm going to do. I propose that we reward your innovations and move you now into our management tier at head office. It's a step up for you. A big step up. It was on the cards for next spring, but now's a better time. It'll prevent this idiot, whoever he or she is, from perhaps going to the Sunday newspapers with sensationalism.'

'But it's all nonsense. I'm delighted at the promotion though. But it's galling that it's to come about like this. If they did that you would sue the paper.'

'I know all that. But believe me Stuart, if these things get that far no one comes out of it smelling of roses. So jump at this chance. OK?'

'Of course! Naturally. And I'm delighted and I am grateful to you.' He thought a moment. 'And I'll be bringing a wife with me; my wife. Not someone else's.'

'Come in Stuart, come right in.' John Cameron ushered him into the manse and along to his study. 'You're no doubt here for the good of your soul, so I've got something that'll do us both a bit of good.' He closed the study door, gestured to a chair, and went over to the desk on which stood a bottle of Glenmorangie single malt whisky and two glasses. 'I imagine you're not teetotal, but take — how do the insurance companies put it — an occasional refreshment?'

Stuart laughed, 'Yes, I take an occasional refreshment.'

'I'm a man of simple tastes when it comes to such refreshments,' and John poured two generous measures. He handed a glass to Stuart. 'First, though, don't you think we should perhaps drink to Willie Meikle?'

Stuart nodded, and smiled.

Both raised their glasses, 'Willie Meikle.'

They sat for a moment. Then John raised his glass, 'Here's to a long and happy marriage.'

They savoured the flavour, then John raised his glass again, 'And here's to your future in senior management.'

They drank to that.

'I would have preferred not to have had a gun put to my head though.'

'Rinse your mind. Some malicious crackpot wants to smear you. But you can't legislate against that sort of thing.' They were both silent for a bit. 'What does Helen feel about it?'

'Really angry that anyone would stoop to that. But after that is said, she takes the same view as you,' and he took another sip of whisky.

'I got some news by phone this afternoon, after your call. Keep it under your hat for the moment. It's not official, but I'll be moving to Glasgow, to take up a teaching post at university.'

'That sounds like congratulations are due,' Stuart said, and raised his glass.

They quaffed again. 'I should have done this sooner. I had my head in the sand. It was when I saw *All Quiet on the Western Front* I realized I had to confront myself.'

'That's interesting,' Stuart said, more animated. 'Lewis Milestone has turned out another winner, *The Front Page*. I've seen reviews. He's excelled with a social and political theme this time.'

They sat silently for a while.

'The real reason I wanted to come round this evening is to ask if you would conduct our wedding?'

'Of course, I would be honoured.'

Stuart pursed his lips. 'I wanted to ask you something. You may have come across it in your parish work.' He paused, and John waited. 'I wonder if there might be a ghost in the marriage, and whether it's a danger?'

'You can't erase the past. The psyche is very complex,' John said. 'If Helen tried too hard to banish what she'd been living with for years, it might lead to guilt. As to whether it's a danger, I think a lot would depend on you. I think in time though, in a marriage, the past would retreat more and more.'

Stuart smiled, and nodded. The whisky's mellow influence soothed them both. 'You're not going to ask me if I've seen the light?'

'Stuart, I've found that if you have seen the light, it's very difficult to keep seeing it.' And he paused, 'The light fades.'

'Helen doesn't want a registry office wedding. She wants it to be carried out by a minister.'

'And you're happy to go along with that?'

'I don't know for sure that there isn't light,' Stuart said.

John recharged Stuart's glass, then his own. 'Let's drink to that.'

It was perhaps a little after this that the sound of singing was heard outside on the road several yards from the windows of the manse study. It sounded, to an elderly couple returning to the town from an evening walk, like the male section of the choir at practice. For the life of them, though, they couldn't place the jaunty tune; they hoped Cameron wasn't going to introduce any revivalist Moody and Sankey jollity. They couldn't be doing with it.

Forty-one years later, Andrew stands looking up at the old cinema. The decades dissolve as he climbs the steps. He had taken over as projectionist when George moved up to be manager after Stuart left. That was it until the start of World War II; after six years service in the RAF, he became cinema manager. In the early sixties, he was appointed Assistant Director at the Scottish Film Council. He was back in his hometown because his mother was failing; she refused to move south; he was arranging a care plan for her.

'It's a sorry sight now, the old cinema. It'll break your heart,' the Worthy had said to Andrew earlier in the day, as he stood waiting for his comrades to gather.

'What's the Worthies take on it in the annals?'

'It gave much pleasure and profit for over thirty years.'

'It's the same all over. Only the big centres can sustain cinemas.'

'Your old boss, Stuart Robertson. Do you ever see him?'

'Regularly. He's retired, but he's a member of the Scottish Film Council. He's a driving force to get the first Regional Film Theatre set up.'

'Is John Cameron, the former minister, still to the fore?'

'He died in March. Stuart, Helen and I were at the funeral. He was buried beside his wife.' Andrew smiled, 'He was a regular filmgoer right up until February.'

'I'll tell the rest of them. It's said by the group that in his last year here, he spent more time at the pictures than at prayer meetings,' the Worthy laughed. 'Well-respected though.'

They had remained standing in silence for a while by the Kenneth Murray memorial.

'You should look in at the old cinema. The building will be open this afternoon. There's an inspection by that body from Edinburgh that takes to do with protecting listed buildings.'

Andrew hesitates on the outside landing. The display units for the stills have been removed. In the foyer, the cashier's box is gutted. Lights are on in the hall, in preparation for the visit. The projection box door yawns, off its hinges. But the two Ross RL projectors are still there. The screen has gone, but the frame remains. There are maybe fifty or so seats left in the stalls. They still look good in their blue plush upholstery.

He retraces his steps. He doesn't want to meet the preservation group. But he returns to the projection box. Man and boy, he'd had Hollywood's golden years here. He shuts his eyes. Which to choose? It takes only a moment: one from the Old Master. Eyes closed, he threads the leader of reel 1 of *Stagecoach* on projector A.

Marilyn's Dead

'Twas on the good ship Venus ...'; or so, at the time, that bawdy rhyme echoed for me, a buttoned-up puritan, travelling deck class by Greek steamer on a quest to the Holy Land. I had just completed an arts degree and was supposed to begin studying for a second degree in divinity in the autumn, but I was going through what was known in the trade at the time as a spiritual crisis.

That early summer of 1962 it had come to a head, thanks to the influence of the new generation of 'God is dead' thinkers, inspired by the French Protestant theologian Gabriel Vahanian.

Until then, mine had been a straightforward faith. I believed in God as Supreme Being, who set down rules for how we should live, and who heard prayer and offered forgiveness. But Vahanian and his ilk were claiming man had left that sort of thinking in the Middle Ages: science can explain the universe and our place in it; we don't need the idea of God as first cause — so far as man is concerned in this post-Christian age, God is dead.

My beliefs had been formed since early teenage years, through church-going, church organisations and activities and my own thinking, until it was put to me that I would be an ideal candidate for divinity. And I'd indeed thought I had a calling.

The worst of it was that the 'God is dead' school going into print were theologians: the Bishop of Woolwich was on his final draft of *Honest to God.* Perhaps if my route to religion had been along the born-again fast lane I would have been impervious to this kind of thinking. But I was open to ideas, and it was undermining my faith. I was afraid I was on a road that would end with me an atheist.

Deeply troubled, I asked for an appointment with the lecturer who was to be my adviser in studies in the Divinity Faculty and told him that I had profound doubts about belief in God.

The divine was in his late thirties, a brisk, no-nonsense Atlas of a man, brimming with bonhomie and exuding robust optimism, who worked out in the university gym and swam in its pool three times a week. You felt he was an adviser with a supportive shoulder. He listened attentively to what I had to say; he came up with no casuistry or counter-thoughts, but picked up his notepad and told me that a trip to the Holy Land in the summer vacation would be 'spiritual reinvigoration' for me. And he beamed, 'Walk the Judean hills that inspired the psalmist, and work the soil that nurtured scripture.' Next he ripped out a page of his notebook with the names of a contact at the American University of Beirut, the warden of a hostel in Jordanian East Jerusalem and the secretary of a kibbutz in Israel. Then he told me to come and see him on the first day of term, 'And we'll have a discussion.' Finally, he held out his hand, gave me an iron grip and sent me on my way.

All well and good, and even exciting to think about; but I had to have funds for such a trip, and even before my religious faith took a tumble I wasn't so naively trusting as to hope that the Lord would provide. But I'd often heard preachers assert that God moves in mysterious ways. And maybe that's what happened. Word got around in my small hometown in the Scottish Highlands about what I was doing, and a businessman, who was an elder of the Kirk, collared me as he was coming out of the bank one morning. He told me that he was a member of a local educational trust and he had found the means to provide me with a bursary that could pay for cheap travel and accommodation in youth hostels.

I was surprised that he had taken the initiative on my behalf: to my mind, he was a worldly-wise character who had not a whiff of the smell of the church hall about him. It seemed to me that every church hall I'd ever been in was designed along the same staid lines, and then its internal walls impregnated with a sacred, fusty compound. And there were certain churchgoers, the ultra-good and the heavy consumers of its activities, whom I associated with the hall's odour. But not him! Indeed, he had jolted me out of an incipient self-satisfaction two years earlier in that very building. I had been dragooned, not altogether unwillingly, into helping a group of the ladies of the church decorate the hall for Christmas. We had worked late into the night, most of the group had left the finishing touches to three of us: two dyed-in-the-wool, compulsive volunteers and myself. And by this time I was feeling I must have been soft in the head to allow myself to have been recruited. The final flourish in transforming the hall was accomplished when the dominant member of the group, an imperious lady in her mid-forties, had me climb the stepladder and fix to the ceiling wide rolls of crimson crepe paper, interspersed with tinsel streamers, letting them drape to the floor to create a flimsy barrier with the main part of the hall. I had just come down the ladder when this elder appeared. He had come to check the electricity meter reading to estimate the charge to be levied on the whist club, that had been in the hall the previous evening. After he took the reading, on his way to the door, he turned to look at the wafting wall of crimson and tinsel; then he came over to me, and with his back to the ladies said in a low voice, 'Reminds me of a brothel in Cairo.'

Momentarily, I was shocked: had I heard what I thought I heard? But then I started laughing and I couldn't stop — my labours, this venue and these respectable ladies whose artistic flair produced such a response! At that he put his hand on my shoulder and drew me towards the door in a friendly fashion so it would appear we were laughing at something between the two of us.

Now for a second time he surprised me with his idea about a bursary to help fund this trip to the Holy Land. He told me to call in at his office the following morning to collect a cheque, which I was then to take to the bank. I duly arrived next day and sat opposite him, and studied my unexpected benefactor as he signed the cheque. He would have been in his early forties, I guessed, with a few grey hairs at the temples. He was about average height, with a wiry build; he had an assured manner, was quiet and undemonstrative, but he gave me the impression he had experienced much that he preferred not to talk about. I held the cheque made out to me, and I saw that the account was in the name of a local educational trust, and that it had two signatures, that of its chairman and that of the church elder, who was its treasurer. He advised me on the amount to take in cash and how much to change into travellers' cheques.

After the episode in the church hall with the Christmas decorations, I'd asked one of his peers, a shopkeeper, with whom he played golf, about his background. He told me that the elder had served in the Commandos during the war, and had seen active service in the Middle East and North Africa and Europe. I recalled seeing him wearing his war decorations at Remembrance parades.

As I was thanking him for the cheque and his thoughtfulness in suggesting the bursary to make the trip possible, it occurred to me to ask, 'Were you in Palestine during the war?'

'Only for a few days.'

'Did you visit any of the religious sites?'

He smiled ruefully, 'It was three days R and R — rest and recuperation — after a raid where we lost a quarter of the unit. So it wasn't the best time to join a crowd of pious wankers.'

I gasped. What did he think about me? So I told him why I was going to the Holy Land and who suggested it: because I had come to have serious doubts about belief in God. He smiled thoughtfully for a moment, looking me over, and then asked, 'How old are you Neil?'

'Twenty-two.'

He nodded, 'The trip may either kill or cure.' Then he raised his eyebrows and gave a quizzical smile, 'And only you will know.'

He certainly had the capacity to surprise me, this pillar of respectability, who spoke his mind. Then his eyes left mine, and I thought at first he was looking out of the window along the High Street, towards the Kenneth Murray memorial, but then I saw that he was gazing into the middle distance; his thoughts were far away. 'How long will you be in Lebanon?' he asked.

'Four days.'

'Four days, that should give you enough time to carry out a small commission for me. For which I'll pay you,' he said. And he added, 'This has nothing to do with the trust.' He took out his wallet and handed across to me a £10 note. 'I would like you to take a bus or a share-taxi from Beirut to the Commonwealth War Graves Cemetery at Sidon. It's not far.' He turned his attention to a pad of paper on this desk and wrote as the spoke. 'There's one grave in particular where I would like you to pay my respects. Pick some poppy anemones. They're plentiful and grow just about everywhere at this time of year out there.' He paused, smiled what I thought was a sad smile, and shook his head, 'He'd talked about going to Jerusalem, if we had a leave in Palestine.' Then he passed over to me the page with the name he'd written. He stood up signalling the end of the transaction, and wished me all the best.

Walking home, I reflected that he must have been about my age when he served with those men who lie buried in Lebanon. They would have known fear — in thrall to the whim of who is chosen and who is passed over by the Angel of Death on the battlefield. By comparison my concerns were self-indulgent. And what awareness did I have of the mystery of life, of grief and loss to be a pastor to others? Perhaps that was the trouble with me — university or not — I wasn't thinking for myself; I was fulfilling the expectations others had of me. I was in an extended childhood. Perhaps this jolt to my beliefs wasn't such a bad thing if it was making me ask questions about myself that I hadn't really faced up to before.

Travelling deck class from Venice to Beirut was the start of a learning curve for me — discovering who I really was, and what I believed in.

With the passing of time, the decade is often referred to as the swinging sixties; but in 1962 its oscillations were not much more than blips in my world. To be sure, the High Court in London had pronounced that *Lady Chatterley's Lover* was not obscene, and although its sales immediately outstripped, so to speak, those of the Bible, it hadn't led, overnight, to wholesale inter-class fornication. True, 'The Pill' had become available on the National Health Service the year before, but only for married women. Legislation allowing abortion lay five years into the future. And condoms were not on display in respectable chemist stores; indeed the term condom was not generally used in those days: they were commonly called French letters. And the French students who converged by rail on Venice and boarded the Greek ship there appeared to have brought a lexicon with them, as well as a hedonistic approach to life.

We all slept close together in our sleeping bags on deck, leaving lanes for the crew to go about their tasks. The first night was chilly in the open air at sea, but I was awakened not by the cold but by sounds of what I realized from the faint light on deck were couples having sex. I was shocked. They had no shame.

It was only on the second day, as the sun came out and we lay around sunbathing, that I started to mingle with one or two of those who were nearest. I happened to find myself near a girl who was in her final year at the École Normale Supérieure, one of the élite grandes écoles. I had fallen asleep in the sun, and when I wakened with the sun burning my back, I saw her sitting alongside a friend. I focused my eyes after sleep; her brown hair, back-lit by the sun, was suffused in an auburn sheen, like the goddess Diana's helmet of burnished bronze. She had finely-drawn features; and she smiled at me with a lovely smile, and I smiled at her; and within a couple of minutes, in French, for I knew more French than she English, we got talking about our studies and our aims for a career. Cécile was going to teach maths in a lycée when she finished her course. She was an atheist and a disciple of Jean-Paul Sartre, so we had some good discussions. Although she was relaxed as a person, she was precise, analytical and, in the French intellectual tradition, rigorously methodical in her thinking.

It was very demanding of my level of French, but later on in the afternoon she led me into less intellectual areas. She brought out a notebook and said with a coy smile, 'Draw a key.'

I said that reminded me of St-Exupéry's *Le Petit Prince*, where the little boy on the new planet says to the airman, "*Dessine-moi un mouton*" (draw me a sheep). What sort of key, a latch-key or one for a mortise lock?'

'You choose.'

I opted for an old fashioned key for a rim lock.

Cécile looked at my drawing and gave an approving smile. Then she said, 'Now draw a glass.'

'What kind of glass?'

'That's up to you.'

I drew a wine glass.

Cécile looked at my efforts, and smiled slyly and said, 'According to Freud, these are sexual symbols: the key represents the male sex organ and the glass the female.'

No girl had ever led me on to the subject of sex within twenty-four hours of meeting her. And Cécile didn't let up the pace.

Next morning, as dawn's fingers were groping across the sea ahead of the ship's bows, I lay on the wooden deck, racked by guilt, surrounded by unseen puritan torturers, punishing me for lewd and lascivious behaviour.

The night before, I had fallen into a deep sleep. I don't know how long I had been asleep, but I wakened, lying on my back, with what felt like a weight across both shins. There was Cécile's head. Before she went to sleep, she had set out her sleeping bag alongside that of a friend of hers and roughly parallel with mine about a metre and a half from me. In the night though, she had wriggled her sleeping bag into an angled position so that her head could reach my legs. She was intent on wakening me.

I responded eagerly. An image of her in panties and cardigan was burned on my mind. Earlier, when she had come from the washroom, to turn in for the night, she was wearing shorts and a fine wool cardigan for the cool night air. She got into her sleeping bag; I stole a glance or two at what followed and memorized every movement. She sat upright, and slipped her arms out of her cardigan, keeping herself covered; she reached up her back and unhooked her bra, and took it off, and put her arms back into the sleeves. Then she lay out inside her sleeping bag and wriggled out off her shorts. She folded the bra and shorts and placed them in the rucksack beside her.

Fumbling in haste, I unzipped her sleeping bag. Her body was warm as I slipped by hands up under her cardigan. I kissed her and felt her rounded breasts. Her nipples became firm under my touch. I was aroused. I was completely inexperienced, but my body urged me further. I moved my hand down over her belly button, anticipating she would stop me. I felt the mound of her pubic hair. A frisson of delight ran up my spine. She placed her hand on mine, moved it, and my fingers became wet. Then she reached out to an open side pocket of her rucksack and handed me a condom.

Never, in my wildest fantasies had I imagined I would be having sex on the open deck of a ship among a group of people. But there was no holding back now, not even if the crew at that moment had sprung a *son et lumière* on us. From the moment she guided me into her; the movement of her pelvis; her soft moaning; the otherness of a young woman utterly consumed me.

The sense of shame I wakened with next morning quickly evaporated as Cécile and I spent time together on deck and in the galley. She simply accepted that giving and receiving the pleasures of the flesh was enriching. And when I thought about it, I realized that this wasn't a modern idea of our post-Christian age. I hadn't the insight when I first read Chaucer to really appreciate the words of the Wife of Bath: 'I have had my world as in my tyme.' She had no regrets about her life, her husbands and lovers; she'd come to terms with the brevity of life and relished experiences as she had them. Cécile knew that too; she lived in the moment. I began to question why God should be against what was natural to us. So why should my religion impose standards of behaviour and condemn what I had done?

For the next four days and nights we were regarded by Cécile's companions as *un couple*; and I grew into a new stage in life. That blissful time, though, was all too short. When the ship put in at Cyprus, it was to be the parting of the ways for a group of French students, who were not going to Beirut but changing to another ship later that day to sail to Haifa. Cécile, an atheist, had no interest in visiting the holy sites in Jordan: she was going to an Israeli kibbutz for ideological reasons; she told me that she wanted to experience at first hand what she took a kibbutz to be: a society based on common ownership, an expression of socialism.

We went to the port side, to the top of the gangway together. We exchanged addresses, but there were no false promises. What we had was for those five days. I watched as she went down the gangway. She waved to me from the quayside. Then she rejoined her group.

Later, in the evening, I stood by the ship's rail near the stern looking westward, as we steamed towards Beirut. The sun was a gigantic orange ball, falling swiftly as though to bounce on the rim of the sea. The air was heady; the scene was intoxicating. I felt freed from the moral fetters of religion. As I stood, the sun shed a fresh cast of colour — and, all at once, I recognized Homer's wine-dark sea. Then the sun slipped from view.

Along with two Americans, Pete and Eric, who had also been on the university campus, I was waiting at the share-taxi rank for the long drive from Beirut, through Syria and then into Jordan and on to Jerusalem. But there would be a break for about an hour in Damascus. This was a standard route for travellers and the driver would set off when he had the allocated number of passengers. Pete and Eric were travelling together on a trip to the Holy Land much like mine, but they were not going to work on a kibbutz, and they were there for a shorter time. They were from a Scandinavian community in Minnesota; Pete was over six feet, fair-haired and broadly built; Eric was darker and slightly shorter in height. Both of them were softly spoken; they were Lutheran; and they faced the prospect of the draft when they finished university. Our driver waited by his taxi. And we stood around.

Beirut had opened a magical window for me into an enchanted part of Asia: vibrant colours, cosmopolitan living; street names in Arabic and French; men sharing a hookah outside a café; eastern souks and modern fashionable stores side by side; men in business suits and men and women in traditional robes; women in summer dresses; girls in jeans or short skirts on the streets, and in bikinis on a sun-scorched beach. Every food stall was a cornucopia, with people bargaining and buying. The American University was set on high ground above the city, and, tracing my way to and from it through the streets, I kept finding another fresh colour knot in the intricate design of an Arabian rug. I walked by a stall selling spices and dried fruits; the aromatic scents in the air were a delight to the nostrils. Another of eastern-style jewellery was an Aladdin's cave that drew me in. And when I was looking for a shawl to take home, the stallholder, with relaxed grace, offered me a glass of tea. Although it was a bustling city, it had dignified charm: elegant mansions were set back from the street; palm-lined drives led to frontages that showed the influence of the different civilisations that were once here, from the classical to the Ottoman period to French colonial. There was a sense of well-integrated styles of living. It was certainly a very different place then from what it became a decade later.

Our taxi was a Ford, and it had had a rough life: big dents in the bodywork, some of which had been crudely beaten out, and a badly twisted rear fender. The driver must have had some instinct that his final passenger would turn up soon, for he signalled to us to put our rucksacks in the boot and pointed us into the rear. I sat at the right hand side behind the front passenger seat. It was ten minutes past ten, and the driver was restlessly talking to one of his colleagues, standing nearby.

At that moment, a priest in a dark suit came trotting up panting to the car with a small case in one hand. He was about forty, although he could have been younger. He got his breath back in gulps, placed his case between his feet, faced the driver, and began talking earnestly. Of medium height, he was pudgy, with small soft hands, which he used constantly, gesturing to the driver. He was scruffy for a cleric; and I thought he had shifty eyes. Without much by way of respect for a man of the cloth, the driver motioned him to sit in the front seat. What happened next was like a sequence from an early silent movie: accelerated action, mime and no dialogue. The priest quickly took in the situation as the driver held the door, and he went rigid, like a rabbit in the middle of the road at night caught in on-coming headlights. Panic-stricken, his soft features were transformed; then he quickly assessed the disposition of the three of us in the back, came up to me in the seat by the door, where I sat with my arm on its window frame, pulled open the door, peremptorily gestured me into the empty front seat without a word. I realized that he wanted to change seats with me. Naturally compliant, I got out and with a smile held the rear door for him to get in, before I took the seat in the front. He ignored me, stood a moment, and, before he got in, he crossed himself. I soon understood why.

After we left the city and had passed through a small village a few kilometres further on, sections of the road surface on the way to Syria were in a state of severe disrepair: large potholes, deep ruts in the surface left by flash-flood water gouging out the bottoming. Without warning oncoming drivers would swing the wheel, lurching their vehicle away from such a hazard, creating scary moments. Car horns blared, expressing anger but to no effect.

I sat for a while running the scenario over in my mind: the irony of a man of God arranging matters so that if there was a crash someone else in the vehicle was more likely to meet his Maker than he. Not a word had been spoken so far by our reverend passenger. As the kilometres were clocked up, my musing began to take a more cynical turn. 'Nearer my God to Thee' was the hymn the passengers of the *Titanic* were supposed to have sung on the deck as they awaited their doom. Then there were standards of conduct that were expected to be observed in life-threatening situations, but this rat in a dog collar would have had a different scale of priority for the vulnerable: women and children and clergy first. I felt angry. There had been chaplains risking their lives in the trenches in the First World War, ministering to the troops; and I'd heard a minister preach who, as its padre, had parachuted into occupied France with his Special Forces unit in the Second World War; but this apology for manhood would never have risked his skin to help others. I sat with the sun beating down on the car and a dry wind from the desert blowing in through the open window, like gusts of hot air from a fan oven baking my anger.

I had to do something. He hadn't said a word to us. Maybe he wasn't at ease with English; based in Lebanon he might be more familiar with French. I knew I would have to keep it simple, and I launched out, and turned right round to face him. 'Are you afraid of death?' I asked in French, with no respectful salutation or acknowledgement of the cloth.

He seemed momentarily taken aback, then he replied swiftly, 'Naturally not. It's the start of eternal life.'

'But are you afraid of the process of dying?'

'I will die when God wills it,' he countered, side-stepping the question.

'Did God will you to sit in the back?'

He gave me a contemptuous scowl. 'God is not mocked, my young man.'

'It wasn't God I was mocking, only his humble servant,' and swung round again. But I knew I hadn't gained a moral victory. And so by the time the Syrian border crossing point loomed up, I was determined to show up this cowardly shepherd of the sheep.

Vehicles had to pull in to one side; you had to get out and join a queue, which tailed back outside the office by the border barrier. My plan was to get through the passport control quickly, and back to the taxi before the priest and reoccupy my original seat in the back.

There seemed to be a separate checkpoint at the side of the building for the taxi drivers, because I didn't see ours again until we were through. The queue forked into two lanes inside the office; and the Syrian uniformed officers were slow, sullen and suspicious with foreigners. Their uniforms were crumpled and ill-fitting; they looked like a bag of washing. They carried automatic pistols in open holsters, and they certainly didn't imbue you with confidence that they were professional. Your passport and visa were scrutinized in great detail by one officer, who at last stamped it; then you were passed to a second officer, and the entire process was repeated in similar detail. I saw the priest in the other line. He must have done this crossing many times before, because when his turn came, he spoke to the first officer in Arabic, gesturing with his tiny hands. The officer checked his papers cursorily, stamped them and passed him on. The second officer was even more dismissive and the priest was through, while I still stood in the queue.

I was fit to be tied. I walked slowly, gritting my teeth. Pete and Eric caught up with me. The taxi stood, doors wide open. The driver was smoking with his back to the vehicle; the priest stood ruminating, secure in his mind that he didn't have to negotiate his place in the car afresh. I still had time to do the dirty on him. 'Quick, into the car,' I said.

'Yeah,' said Pete, getting the idea, 'he's chicken-shit,' and, grinning, nudged Eric. They got into the back seat and I jumped in too.

The priest was caught unawares. He came up to the taxi on my side, put his nicotine-stained fingers on the bodywork through the open window, and looked at me long. I held his gaze. He had known

113

instinctively when he joined us that I was the soft touch, the easy mark, who was only too happy to please. And he simply knew he would get no change out of the other two, who sat in complete indifference to it all. He exhaled, turned around and climbed into the front seat. The driver switched on the ignition, and we drove off into Syria.

I relished watching the passenger in front of me. I sat anticipating when he would react. I felt malevolent glee as every now and then his shoulders tensed, and I sensed he braced his feet against the floor. Further on, I watched his left hand gripping the edge of his seat as our driver overtook another car, and swerved back onto our own side in the face of an on-coming car with its horn blaring. The priest was a quivering jelly.

Suddenly, everything changed! It all happened in an instant without warning: I too, like Saul of Tarsus, had a road to Damascus experience. But in my case, I saw clearly; it was as though scales fell from my eyes, and I realized what I was really doing. I was punishing myself when I excoriated him. This poor priest was scapegoat for my own weakness. I didn't have his fear of the front seat, but I had lost my confidence in who I was and where I was going in life. I had been wallowing in self-pity for allowing myself to be shoehorned into divinity studies: of simple faith, diligent, compliant, presentable in public, a good fit for the ministry. And at the first challenge from contrary-minded theologians I buckled at the knees.

I was in no position to judge whether the priest was craven or brave. He might be the equivalent of the shell-shocked veteran going over the top again. He may have had to do the journey so often it turned him into a mental wreck, steeling himself each time. I remembered the whisky priest in Graham Greene's *The Power and The Glory*, a pathetic, frightened figure who yet had spiritual grace surrounding him. A wave of compassion for this priest broke over me.

A cacophony of blaring horns distracted me. The road ahead was an uphill incline. In our lane an old jalopy of a van had collapsed, its rear nearside wheel tilted at an acute angle to its axle. Men had got out of their vehicles; there was much noise and shouting. Traffic in our lane slowed to a crawl. Finally our driver had to stop. Without thinking, I opened my door, sprang out, yanked open the front passenger door, jabbed two fingers in the air towards the startled priest, and pointed him into the rear seat. His eyes were wary. I realized he expected me to torment him further and he refused to allow himself to move. I leaned into the car, took him by the lapels of his black jacket, and pulled him out of his seat. He went limp. I read naked fear in his eyes. That made it worse for me. But I couldn't delay, and I pulled him with me to the rear door and shoved him into the car. I took his place in the front. Not a word had been spoken by either of us. A few men rolled the broken down van off the road, and our lane moved again.

I settled into the erratic style of our driver once more. The hot, arid scrubland acted like a sedative. I became relaxed. Certainly, mine wasn't of the same magnitude on the Richter scale as Saul's, but my experience was nonetheless transformative: by feeling pity for the priest I eased up on scourging myself. *OK, just accept*, I told myself, *we all have our weaknesses as well as strengths.* I would go with the flow on this quest and see where it took me.

By the time we reached Damascus, I felt serene; like British royalty, I could have given a regal wave from the taxi to whomsoever.

That first sight of Jerusalem's Old City from the front seat of the share-taxi quickened my pulse. From early childhood it had been a name with mystical associations in stories, hymns and poetry. And now, ahead of me, the golden Dome of the Rock glistened in the bright sun, the Temple Mount, parts of the crenellated old wall and a myriad of flat, white roofs reflected light, and buildings swept higgledy-piggledy down from the contour of the hills. Years later I saw the painting 'Allenby Before Jerusalem' which depicts General Allenby on horseback, his hand on the horse's croup, pausing before the city he is soon to enter, the city he had wrested from Ottoman rule in the decisive battle of 1917. A file of troops heads downhill to its walls. Although, in the painter's pose, Allenby is the victorious general observing his army moving towards the city's walls, when, a little later on that December day 1917, he himself reached the walls, he adopted the status of a pilgrim, and dismounted, and went on foot through the Jaffa Gate into the city. Although the battle paved the way for the British Mandate, that painting is a thumbnail for the history of the Holy City, the city venerated by Jew, Christian and Moslem, the city that was fought over for hundreds of years and is still being fought over.

Pete, Eric and I agreed to meet during the week and go to the Dead Sea. Then we went our several ways: Pete and Eric to a hotel that had been booked for them, I to a hostel I'd already written to, and the priest — God knows where.

A young Arab man was on duty at the hostel. He took my passport and told me that when I was settled in the warden would like to see me in his office. I showered and changed, and then I knocked on the office door.

The warden gave me a friendly welcome and invited me into his spacious office, and then he immediately offered me Arabic coffee. He was a Christian Arab; he said that he and the academic at my university, who prompted my trip, had both been tutors at a summer school a few years back. I slowly sipped and savoured the coffee, with the lovely flavour of cardamom. The office was functional but it also had a leather sofa and two leather chairs. An Arabian rug hanging on the wall facing the window immediately caught your attention. It was a work of great craftsmanship; it absorbed the light and drew you into an ornate design; the colours danced together in an intricate ritual. The warden was in his early forties. He was slightly portly, and a family man, with a photo of his two young children on his desk. He was efficient, precise in his language; and he struck me as a thoughtful man who measured his words as he spoke. He didn't go into the background of the divided city or the politics of the situation, but he may have looked on what he was doing as providing a two-part learning experience for me: one part seminar and the other field work with a tutor. But he acted more like a genial host than the senior executive of an organisation. And he showed me the ropes for crossing into Israel: the required number of days I'd have to stay in Jordan first; directions to the official office in a backstreet for the exit papers authorizing my crossing; and the procedure at Jerusalem's Mandelbaum Gate — the only route that was open from an Arab country into Israel.

Then he leaned back in his chair and said, 'A guide would be useful to you for part of the time you'll be in East Jerusalem. There's a young man we're helping through college. Jamal is his name, he's a Palestinian. He's seventeen and is about to begin a course in a technical college. He could be your guide for three days; after that he is committed to working in a cousin's store.'

The warden must have read an anxious expression on my face.

'Jamal will not accept payment. He wants to practise his English.'

I smiled a smile of relief, 'That would be a big help.'

Jamal was waiting for me in the entrance next morning, and the warden's assistant introduced us. Jamal had a friendly face; he was about five feet six, slim with high cheek-bones and his eyes lit up in a sparkling smile. We got on right from the start.

We walked the narrow alleys of the Old City that were vibrant with life. And it wasn't a blending of the old and the new, as it had been in Beirut, it felt more like continuity with past centuries. The Wife of Bath had made three pilgrimages to Jerusalem, Chaucer tells us; if she re-materialized in the flesh in the mid-twentieth century and came here on a fourth, she would have found her way around the narrow streets of the Old City as she had over half a millennium ago. There was a stall of leatherwork next to what Jamal said was an Armenian jewellery maker; there was pottery, and there was a stallholder selling silks almost next to one selling butchered meat, and there was a spice market; the narrow alleys were alive with the sounds of traders calling, and there were exotic smells and strange sights. There was a stone fountain with two tiers that lapped water into a fairly shallow trough; the trough was half-full of water from which a donkey was drinking while its owner stood beside it and removed his sandals; then, holding on to the donkey's rump and standing on one leg, he leisurely soaked first one foot and then the other in the drinking water. I responded to Jerusalem's old streets with the enthusiasm of a small boy; and I quite forgot the reason for my being there.

Jamal had an infectious laugh. His English was quite good and he was keen to practise it and improve; and so we kept a dialogue flowing as we walked. He would use an expression, and I would suggest an alternative, more appropriate one in the context; he certainly believed in experimenting with language and breaking new ground. Sometimes it was hilarious. But then he suddenly unnerved me when he held my hand as we walked.

What the hell's this? I thought, and I instantly withdrew my hand and looked at him. He must have read aggression from my eyes. He was taken aback and said nothing. I had seen Arab men and teenage boys walking hand in hand. It must have been a sign that he felt we were bonding; but it was too much for me. He sensed that there were different norms in my culture, and he was sensitive; he didn't try to explore that through language.

If the purpose of this quest to the Holy Land was to resuscitate my expiring faith, I shouldn't have been reluctant to begin a circuit of the religious sites. But I dithered when Jamal kept asking when I was going to make a start. When I'd been in Lebanon, I'd gone to Baalbek's ancient Roman ruins that lay in a flat valley floor between two ranges of hills. The sun beat down mercilessly as I walked from the road towards the awe-inspiring six pillars of the temple of Jupiter. Their height was astonishing, their builders aspiring to the idea of the Immortals. Much more remained of the temple of Bacchus; and the third temple, when I read the sign, made me smile: it was dedicated to the goddess Venus. The ancient gods had human characteristics and desires. But now those gods are dead. And some theologians had written the obituary of the God that superseded them. Would our churches and cathedrals end up like Baalbek's temples I wondered?

Perhaps that thought made me reluctant to face a round of the Christian sites. But I couldn't keep putting it off.

We made our way towards the Church of the Holy Sepulchre. Jamal said that he would wait outside for me.

'I hope you don't get into a fight,' he said.

'An argument you mean?' There was a smile on his face, but I couldn't interpret it.

'No a fight with fists,' and he clenched his fists.

I shook my head, not understanding. It didn't make sense, 'You're joking,' I said.

'No,' he laughed, 'the holy men had a fight once there. The police had to go in and stop them.' He opened his arms, made a gesture; I read it as what do you make of that? Then he shrugged, 'The holy men.' He turned on the spot, and with one foot idly kicked his other foot.

I joined a large crowd heading into the church. I hadn't really given any credence to what Jamal was saying. It must have been what he had heard, or there was a rumour and it became magnified in the retelling.

The vast interior was much darker than I expected. As I stood to let my eyes become accustomed to the gloom, I was almost bowled over by a man in a monk's garb, leading a group of people at an urgent pace to wherever they were going. The building was full of people. There was heaviness of incense in the air; and now and again as I moved further in, the rank smell of human flesh, as though the building hadn't been aired for centuries. I skirted round the fringes of the groups, looking at the ornamentation, the icons, the silver and gold decoration.

Groups of people, usually led by a cleric, moved to their different altars. The Church of the Holy

Sepulchre underlined for me the splits in Christianity; and each persuasion was insistent it held the truth — a section for the Orthodox, another for the Catholic; there were Copts and there were Armenians.

The religious leaders of the various groups looked intense; there was what I took to be a claim of right to their allocated altar. I could imagine tempers getting frayed among the faithful. Traditions had developed, and the church held the accretions of the ages. But the site itself was of dubious authenticity. I moved towards the exit, feeling disenchanted.

When I emerged into the bright light, I tried to get my bearings, but Jamal saw me and came across. I could have given up the idea of further visits there and then. But he had been primed to show me the Christian sites, and that he did. Until I had had enough. And two days of it were more than enough.

The only Christian site that had some interest for me was the Garden Tomb. It was a rock escarpment outside the Old City walls. The shape of the rock face with its caves could be said to match the New Testament description of Golgotha, the place of the skull. A much quieter place that didn't attract many visitors, it may have been no more the place where Jesus was buried than was the Church of the Holy Sepulchre; but it showed the kind of burial place a rich man might have had way back in time.

Fighting over who could pray where wasn't restricted to Christianity: Jews were forbidden access to their holy places in the Jordanian part of the city; and in their disagreements Jews and Moslems used live ammunition. More and more it was borne in on me, as we continued walking, that we invented our religions. And in time, we would discard them.

It was much better having Jamal with me than exploring on my own. He didn't have an itinerary for me; I simply took my time from the travellers' guidebook and he led the way. We had gone beyond the walls of the Old City, and Jamal was pointing out something to me.

'Can you point out the dividing line between Jordan and Israel?' I asked.

'The Israelis,' he said, drawing out each of the two middle vowels, 'are over there,' he said, pointing in the general direction. 'We don't say Israel. We don't accept it is a state.'

'Why is that, do they not have a right to be here too?'

'No, in 1948 they took our land, the land of our forefathers, and drove us out.'

'I don't know the recent past, but in Old Testament times the Jews were here.'

'But it was ours,' and he stopped abruptly at that. From Jamal's response I wasn't sure whether he agreed with what I'd said or not. It was all very well, though, for me, a foreigner, to take an objective view; I wasn't one of the dispossessed. I tried to empathize with his situation; even if you were only a child in 1948 when you left you would harbour resentment about your family's loss. I didn't have enough background into what happened, so I thought it was perhaps better to leave questions unasked.

Jamal knew, though, that I was going into Israel. It was a strange situation in East Jerusalem: no Arab country recognized Israel, yet tourism was important for the economy, and tourists and pilgrims wanted to see sites that were in both Jordan and Israel; so the compromise was a discreet, side street office where visitors — so long as they were not Jews (you had to produce certification from a recognized church, or some legal authority stating your religion) — received a visa, after having been in Jordan for a week, allowing them to pass through the Mandelbaum Gate into Israel.

We left any thoughts on that unspoken. We were going our different ways, whatever they turned out to be; and we had a sincere, almost emotional farewell, and wished each other well for the future.

That evening, when I asked the warden about the division between the two states. He smiled, 'Did Jamal speak to you about it?'

'Yes, when I asked him, he didn't accept that Israel exits, and said that his family were forced to flee in 1948.'

'For the Palestinians that was the *nabka*, the catastrophe, when the state of Israel was formed.'

'Were they forced to flee their land?'

'Some were; some fled of their own accord, expecting reprisals if they didn't; and some stayed.'

'Can't both Palestinians and Israelis co-exist?'

'In theory, yes. In reality, it's doubtful. It would need leadership, and leaders have to find ways of expressing what their followers believe. And Arabs are proud people.' He shook his head, 'So it is not going to happen quickly.' He looked at me and smiled, 'You may think it strange for a Christian to think like that.' Then he shrugged, 'Maybe. Maybe, some day.'

The sunlight, filtered by a gossamer of smoke-grey cloud, set off the arid hillsides and the green waters of the Dead Sea. Eric, Pete and I had arranged to meet at the bus station and take a local bus south from Jerusalem for some relaxation in an unusual setting. I found that they had reacted to the Holy City like a relaxed pair of tourists; they'd taken it all in their stride. But I was glad to get away from man-made religious sites and the negative thoughts they triggered in me.

We floated in the lake, each of us coming out in turn to take photos of the other two. By the time we got dried, there was a thick saline deposit on the camera cases from our wet hands.

I had another reason too for coming here: I wanted to get an impression of the Judean desert where the Dead Sea Scrolls had been found in sealed up caves. The hostel warden had told me that we wouldn't be allowed into the area where the digging was still going on, but I was keen to come, nonetheless.

The scrolls, I'd learned from students at the Divinity Faculty, were thought to be the work of the Quram Essenes, a Jewish sect who followed an ascetic life. Some of the parchment and papyrus scrolls were written before the Christian era. They had been marvellously preserved thanks to the very dry air here. Already, some French scholars had published their early findings. So far, though, there was no reference to Jesus in the scrolls. But there was still a lot of work to be translated.

This strange place that nature created made a strong impact on me; perhaps in the same way it had fascinated people throughout the ages. King David had a refuge here; the Essenes lived in caves in the hills here, and others before them. Maybe that was the only way to live a life in the mind. But it was thought to have bodily health benefits as well. And today a few Jordanians were taking cures in its waters.

A sign in English and Arabic said that this was the lowest point on the earth's surface.

I stood apart for a bit, deep in thought, looking at the green-tinged mirror of the Dead Sea. And as I stood the mirror seemed to reflect to me a truth I didn't really want to face. But I had to. The river Jordan was such an important symbol in the Old Testament; John the Baptist baptized Jesus with its water; and it was fabled in song. I ran a couple of lines of the lyric from the spiritual 'Michael Row the Boat Ashore' through my head:

Jordan's river is chilly and cold, hallelujah,
Chills the body but not the soul, hallelujah

But the truth the mirror of the waters told is that the river Jordan ends its course flowing not into a sea teaming with life, but a dead lake with no outlet, and there evaporates. It was the same with faith, I thought. From polytheism to monotheism, they end up in the cesspool of dead beliefs. I had reached my spiritual nadir. I had to accept the sad truth: I was losing my remaining faith.

Perhaps it was because I was low and feeling emotionally vulnerable, but something happened on the way back to Jerusalem that spoke to my soul from a faraway land.

There were only about seven or eight people on the local bus. Pete and Eric were sitting across the passageway from me. The driver had the vehicle's radio playing Arabic music at a reasonable volume. An announcer's voice came on. There was a double drum roll followed by the first sounds from the drones of the great Highland bagpipe and then the opening bars of a two/four march.

I was gripped by a sudden surge of emotion. I swallowed hard, and took a deep breath, '"The Barren Rocks of Aden,"' I said across the passageway to Pete. He looked puzzled. 'The tune, it's called "The Barren Rocks of Aden", a place on the Red Sea. It was composed in the last century. A Highland regiment was based there. Must be the pipe band of the Royal Jordanian Army. I've seen them at the military tattoo at Edinburgh Castle.'

'Pipes and drums out here?' said Pete.

'British army-trained,' I said.

'Yeah?'

'Yes, British officers used to train their forerunners, the Arab Legion. And King Hussein, Jordan's king, went to officer training school in the UK.'

'I thought you were interested in theology, but you seem to be up on the military,' Pete said.

He was right. I had mastered the fingering of that tune as a boy in primary school when I learned to play the pipe chanter, because it was the most natural thing for a youngster in my part of the world, at that time, to have a keen interest in all things military. The Second World War was of recent memory and most men in the area had served in the forces. And that had been my ambition too, when I was in primary school. All that was before . . .

When I was in first year at university, the country still had National Service. Like Eric and Pete, I'd anticipated being called up after my arts degree; I would have military experience before the next step. But then the government discontinued National Service two years before my turn would have come.

'Yes, but no problem. It's a case of "praise the Lord and pass the ammunition,"' I said.

Eric grinned broadly, and said, 'It's been that way too with us in the States. Have you seen John Ford's Western *The Searchers*?'

'Yes, great film.'

'Remember the scene where the file of Texas Rangers is flanked on both sides by the Indians, following them and about to attack? The captain of the Rangers is a clergyman. And the John Wayne character says to him, "Well, it looks as though you got yourself surrounded Reverend."'

Pete and I were both laughing, when Eric went on, 'And do you remember what the Reverend replied? "Yeah, and I reckon on getting myself unsurrounded."'

I wondered what was to come next.

'Well he wasn't going to pray about it to get them "unsurrounded", he was going to fight a way out,' Eric said, chuckling.

We discussed the merits of Westerns, and what they depicted of the Old Frontier until we arrived at the bus station. It was a parting of the ways, for this was to be my last night in East Jerusalem.

I approached the Mandelbaum Gate with my rucksack on my back. It was Sunday, a little after 9am. I had spent the requisite number of days in Jordan; my passport and papers were checked by the Jordanian authorities; and I passed through and walked the few yards on the other side into Israel and presented them to the Israeli official. He asked me how long I would be staying in Israel; and I told him it would be for two months. He handed my passport back, and I set off walking the 4 or 5 kilometres south of the Mandelbaum Gate to my first destination before taking a bus to Tiberias.

My port of call was another religious building. I was going to a church that had been built during the British Mandate as a memorial to the Scottish soldiers killed bringing Ottoman rule in Palestine to an end. And I was not going reluctantly, because this had nothing to do with faith or lack of it: I had given myself a duty to perform. I was heading for the Sunday morning service at St Andrew's Scots Church, just inside Israel and very close to the 'Green Line', the cease-fire line between Jordan and Israel. During the 1948 war of Independence the church had often been hit by gunfire, and the minister of the time raised the Saltire, the Scottish flag, from the church tower, hoping to spare the building from greater damage.

I heard what sounded like the staccato cracking of a car back-firing from the direction in which I was heading. It wasn't long before I could see the Saltire draped on the flagstaff of the church tower in the still air. A stretch of open ground lay ahead bounded by a fence, and then it dipped out of sight.

But then, all of a sudden, I became very alert. It was as if something in the air reverberated, and my senses were pitched at a higher level. Ahead of me, a little way to the right of the church, a knot of people had formed. I guessed that the open ground, which sloped out of sight and then rose up into what must be Jordanian territory, was the Hinnom Valley; the cease-fire line ran through the middle of it, and on either side of it was an area bordered by a fence. What I'd seen from a distance was the fence on the Israeli side, and the area on the other side of it was No Man's Land. Anyone venturing into it risked being shot by either side. I couldn't see any activity on the Jordanian side, but on the Israeli side, directly ahead of me, an ambulance bearing the Red Shield of David drew up; a medical orderly held high a white flag and waved it in wide arcs. The rear doors of the ambulance stood wide open. Then with slow, deliberate movements, two stretcher-bearers approached the fence. They waited briefly, and slipped through the fence while another man held two strands of barbed wire wide apart. I had a tight feeling in my stomach. The stretcher-bearers disappeared, and then reappeared, carrying first one, and then a second stretcher on which was a wounded or dead serviceman. Then the ambulance sped away. The whole process from its arrival until its departure couldn't have taken more than four minutes.

As I came nearer I saw that people were beginning to move into the church. One of the men, an office-bearer I assumed, stepped forward to welcome me. He held out his hand, and before I could ask him, he said, 'Two Israeli soldiers crossed through the fence into No Man's Land. They posed, taking photos of each other. The Jordanians opened up from a gun placement.'

The gunfire could have been what I took to be a car engine in need of tuning.

'Pointless,' he said. 'Doing it for a dare.'

Silently we walked into the vestibule. According to the plaque on the wall, building work for the church began in 1927. Allenby, the soldier who had led the British army in the battle for Jerusalem ten years earlier, laid the foundation stone 'in commemoration of the liberation of Jerusalem on 9th December 1917.' That liberation lasted only thirty-one years.

In the service that morning, the minister sensitively included in his prayer the two young men, perhaps displaying an innocence that they might not be a target because they meant no harm. But even as he uttered those sentiments, I knew that there was another side to it: you are responsible for your decisions, and they were culpable; they had disobeyed their army's standing orders and put themselves needlessly at risk. The Roman centurion's words in the New Testament story mirrored a soldier's thinking when he said to Jesus, 'speak the word only, and my servant shall be healed', because military orders are to be obeyed.

During the sermon, I lost interest. I thought about my reason for coming to the church. Before the service began, I'd signed the visitors' book; then I wrote, In Memory of — — and inserted the name of the man on whose grave at Sidon I had placed flowers, the man who had wanted to spend a leave in Jerusalem, but whose life had been cut short by war.

Fulfilling the commission given to me by the church elder, I had taken a share-taxi from Beirut to Sidon. From the coast road, the sea had been a shimmering sheet of cobalt, the eternal surge of its breakers sighing along the shore. And I sat with a spray of flowers that included poppy anemones, bought from a stallholder. The Commonwealth War Cemetery at Sidon was not a vast war cemetery on the lines of those in Europe: neat rows of close on two hundred gravestones; the resting place of the men of No. 11 (Scottish) Commando who fell at the raid on the fortifications at the Litani river. They were all so young. The lieutenant colonel in charge of the unit was only thirty-six. The man at whose grave I placed the spray on behalf of the veteran back home had been my age.

I hadn't known, until that visit, that when the commandos ran from their landing craft that June morning in 1941 their enemy was Vichy France; they fired on the flag of France, their former ally; and Lebanon did not exist as a state at that time; it was part of Syria. The vagaries of politics! Now, the enemies here were Arab and Israeli.

For a long stretch of the 100 or so kilometre journey to Tiberias I was preoccupied with a perplexing thought: perhaps God did not exist, but evil existed. The proof of it was all around. The bus driver was of European origin, and so were most of the passengers. Since the start of the century, Jews had been returning to Palestine in large numbers for the first time since the Diaspora, escaping from anti-Semitism in Europe — Christian Europe.

And all that was before the Nazis plumbed the abyss of man's inhumanity to man. A few weeks before I left home, Adolf Eichmann had been executed in this land of Israel for crimes against humanity. Newspapers in the UK had splashed the news that he had been captured in Argentina by Israeli agents. It sounded wildly exaggerated. But then the trial began. In my student digs we didn't have a TV, but we had a radio. The first item on the 6 o'clock news that evening was the recorded words of the prosecuting attorney asking the defendant his identity:

'*Sind Sie Adolf Eichmann?*'

And the snapping, two-syllable reply, '*Jahwol*.'

There he was on trial in the land that was the cradle of monotheism, a key administrator of state-sanctioned crime, the Holocaust.

But the demons Adolf Hitler released from Berlin had willing helpers in other countries: next month, July, would be the twentieth anniversary of the French police rounding up 13,000 Jews, men, women and children and herding them into the Vél d'Hiv, the Vélodrome d'Hiver, in Paris. They were to be transported in cattle trucks to Auschwitz. Cécile told me on board ship, in a diatribe against French government policy — and President De Gaulle, former leader of the Free French (*le grand Charles*, she called him) — that the twentieth anniversary of the Vél d'Hiv would not be officially remembered in Paris; it was not taught in the curriculum in French schools. Politicians did not want the young to learn of the crimes of their fathers. It would have been no different in Britain, if we had been invaded. Despite our jingoism now, we too would have had our share of guilt. There was no hope for us.

I tried to let the bus journey bring my spirits up a bit. There were signs of human endeavour everywhere. The countryside was much more heavily cultivated than it was just a few miles east in Jordan: wheat had been harvested; there were citrus groves in abundance; and tractors were working in the fields.

The driver of the bus from Tiberias to Safed dropped me at the road end of the kibbutz. It was set by the shores of the Sea of Galilee. In Hebrew the lake is called Kinneret. I walked down a narrow tree-lined road. There was a faint aromatic scent here and there, but I couldn't identify the trees. Then I reached a point where the air became redolent of approaching a farm steading. There was a silo and there was the distinctive smell of cattle as I passed a large byre.

A sign in Hebrew and English pointed the way to the administration block. Low, single-storey dwellings lined the roadway to the block. The lady who was on duty in the office was in her late forties, with streaks of grey running through her hair, which was tied up in a bun. She had a pleasant, open mien that reminded me of a type of woman I'd come across before. 'I'm Esther,' she said. This, I found, was the practice; there was no formality: given names only were used. She told me that she had been expecting me around this time, and she appeared to be in no rush to get rid of me and back to her work, as she was filing away my passport. Her English was very fluent and had the inflexion of a native German speaker.

She asked me about my studies; then to my surprise mentioned two or three European writers and wondered if I had read them in translation or the original. One I had. Well, well, I thought, not the sort of discussion you were likely to hear in a farmhouse kitchen back home.

When I thought it was my turn, I asked her, 'When was the kibbutz founded?'

'It was in 1936/37,' she said with a faint smile.

'And the original founding members were from different countries in Europe or mainly one?'

'The first group of us were Austrian, soon some others came from Germany.'

I felt it would be tactless and needless to pursue that further, so I said, 'You chose a lovely place and you've an attractive lay-out of chalets.'

She gave a rueful laugh, 'It was swampland when we came here. We had to drain it. And we lived in tents. Yes,' she said in response to my raised eyebrows, 'away back at the beginning our accommodation was under canvas.'

'How long did it take to create what you have now?'

'We did it in phases, the second phase of accommodation was wooden huts. You'll be living in one of them. We didn't get rid of all of them.' And she laughed, 'You'll find out how hot it gets in a wooden building.'

She may have felt that was enough by way of an introduction to the kibbutz, for she said, 'You will be allocated to work in the banana plantation. Reuben is in charge. Be at the dining hall this evening at 5.45 and Reuben will meet you and give you the details of when you begin in the morning and where you'll be picked up.' Then she looked me over, 'Do you have clothes you can work in?'

'Yes, I think I'm all right on that.'

She gave me the key with the number of my abode, came to the office door and pointed out the way to the dining hall and the toilets and showers.

The wooden buildings that remained were set back off the metalled paths that led to the newer generation of buildings. I found my semi-detached hut, really, of well-weathered timber cladding. All it amounted to was the sleeping area for an individual or a couple; ablutions and eating were part of the communal life; and so was child-rearing. It was the secret of the progress they'd made in twenty-five years. Mercifully, the pitched roof was not covered in corrugated iron or it would have been an oven.

So this was to be home for two months; I would be working in a sharing community with descendants of Jews who had been here before the Diaspora.

Darkness had fallen when I arrived at the dining hall. A broad-shouldered man in a blue-checked short sleeve shirt was talking to two men just inside the hall, and I saw him register my presence. I stood by the entrance and in a moment or two, when he had finished talking to them, he came over to me, held out his hand, and in a distinctly American accent said, 'You're our volunteer from Scotland.'

'Yes, I'm here for two months.'

'And you're not afraid of hard work?' he asked with a smile.

'No,' I said, 'and I'm ready for it.'

He laughed, 'Good. We begin at 4am. Arrive here no later than 3.45, there's an urn of tea. We leave by truck and go to the fields, about fifteen minutes. Don't worry, we'll be picked up from the fields at 8am and taken back here for breakfast, then return to work until noon. Then we finish and come here for lunch. The rest of the day's your own.' And he gestured into the hall, 'Have your meal.' But he didn't join me.

The dining hall was busy. You just took a seat at one of the long tables; I sat beside one of the men Reuben had been talking to. We didn't speak but nodded to each other. It was like school dinners in lay out. But I soon found out that it was a much healthier diet than anything school meals staff ever dished up. Bowls of salad were already on the tables; those who were on duty in the dining hall came round with trolleys and you made your choices. From that first meal on I knew that table manners were not a high priority: you simply reached for what you wanted and didn't waste words asking someone to pass it to you.

After his glucose level had been spiked, the companion on my right, who had been talking to Reuben, noticing that I had gone for the fish from the menu, suddenly broke into fluent English, 'We try to be as self-sufficient as possible. Anyway, too much red meat's not good for you.'

I smiled and nodded, but I felt he was rationalizing. Years later, I learned they were ahead of their time.

Next morning, it was still dark at 3.35 when I left the hut. I was teamed with a group of eight men of varying ages, from their early twenties to mid forties. Other teams already knew their grouping; and our team climbed into the back of a truck and we drove off, crossed the highway running north/south and in ten minutes reached our destination. There was by now enough light to walk from a main track along the rows of banana trees where we were to work. The charge-hand took me to my row of trees, handed me a saw-toothed curved knife with a wooden handle, and demonstrated how he wanted me to cut off the outer leaves of the sheath surrounding the main stem quite close to the ground. Removing the old leaves helped concentrate the tree's energy to the higher fruit-bearing parts. Having cut off the leaves, you threw them to the side of a wide avenue that ran parallel with every fifth row of plants, and along which a tractor could pass. He watched me cut the leaves of two or three trees, nodded and said in English that it was OK.

It was not difficult work, but you had to be careful not to cut deeper than the outer leaves and slice into the stem and reduce the flow of nutrients from the roots; and you had to keep up a good pace, because you could see the progress others were making in their rows. They were experienced and had long ago learned the knack whereas I was expending needless effort in the broiling sun. Bent double under the broad flat leaves higher up the plant, you were not in direct sun all the time, but it was demanding of your endurance, and soon it was back-breaking.

After what felt like hours, the charge-hand of the group called out in Hebrew and the others stopped where they were, left their tools at the point they had reached and began walking to the main track. One of them gave me in English the magic words — water break. We gathered round a plastic water butt that had been dropped off earlier from a jeep, and we filled for ourselves one of the half dozen aluminium mugs. We sat around and rested for five minutes. It was comradely, grouped round the water butt. To begin with, though, they didn't engage with me. Then after three or four days there was a sudden thawing in their attitude to me. I realized that the kibbutznikim were accepting me because I didn't shirk, I worked as best I could.

Even though I felt I would never stand up straight again, I couldn't but be impressed by the scientific approach they'd taken to obtaining the highest yield. Not too many of the earlier founders of the kibbutz could have had much experience of cultivating bananas, yet they had worked out the best method in their situation. The water source was Kinneret; and from a dam they flooded the growing area in the evening. But it was the way they did it that impressed me. There were concrete-lined ditches calibrated to allow the exact volume of water per hour that experience (or expert advice from abroad) showed benefited the plants. By first light, when we arrived to work, the water had been absorbed into the soil; the only signs that remained of its presence were the wet dead leaves by the side of the track.

A regime unfolded of work, sleeping in the early afternoon until the heat of the day had passed, then swimming in the Sea of Galilee, and in the evening relaxing in the community or culture centre. This was a two-storey building, and it was a focal point for the community with a library, magazines, newspapers, including the English language *The Jerusalem Post*, and rooms where talks or lectures could be given.

As a boy, I loathed the Highland Sabbath with its minatory thou shalt nots: no sports, no cinema, no joy; but I was now ready to concede that the Almighty had such a good idea in ordaining six days for work and the seventh for rest, because Shabbat was pure bliss. It was the only day we had free, and it began, as the Jewish Sabbath does, on the Friday evening. For the Shabbat evening meal, shirts were crisper and, more often than on week-days, they were white, as though white was for best; women's dresses were attractive, slightly more formal, less casual than during the week. But there was no religious element to the evening meal; and no one on the kibbutz, I learned, attended synagogue; it was very much a secular community. And Shabbat was its day of rest.

Life wasn't entirely a modern day idyll though. One night on my way back to my hut from the culture block, I saw our armed guard. He patrolled the paths of the living quarters, armed with what looked like a British army thirty-eight pattern webbing holster, so the pistol butt was concealed by the button-down flap. Military service was compulsory for men and women. The reality was that the Arab states considered themselves still in a state of war with Israel; there was a cease-fire, not a peace treaty. Palestine Fedayeen carried out raids into Israel. They were not large-scale raids, according to the reports I read in *The Jerusalem Post*. Nor, at that time, were the Fedayeen armed with much more than small arms — though occasionally hand grenades. And the usual pattern of the incursions over previous years was isolated killings.

After about a week, I got into the swing of the work regime. I had no money worries; it was almost a currency-free community. You earned your keep by the sweat of your brow. And it was a world away from being self-absorbed in the mind. I really began to relish the practical life, and I had the satisfaction of doing work more meritorious and essential — according to Jonathan Swift — than the efforts of all politicians put together: making two ears of corn or two blades of grass grow where one grew before.

The young Sabras of the kibbutz, those Israelis who were born in Palestine, were reserved with an outsider. There were some lovely girls, but they didn't show any sign of wanting to interact with me. I wished it had been otherwise, but there was nothing coming to me from any of them.

One of the young men, Amos, and I gravitated together though. He was about my age, and he'd completed his military service, and he was keen to talk about kibbutz life and living in general. He told me the name Sabra came from a very thorny plant which has a soft inside; the young Israelis had a tough exterior but were softer underneath.

Reuben's job was manager of the banana plantation, so he had administrative duties as well as oversight of the various fields covering a wide area making up the plantation. He would often come to the fields. He turned up at a water break and he came over to talk to me. He was about five feet eleven, in his early to mid-forties and he had a relaxed style about him.

'You're used to manual work,' he said in his American accent. So he had heard that I tried to keep my end up with the rest of the team.

'Yes I've done manual work, when I was at school and at university.' I felt emboldened, 'You didn't come from Europe to the kibbutz?'

'I was born in the States. My parents came to Palestine when I was twelve,' he said. 'What brought you to Israel?'

'Well, next term, I was supposed to begin studying theology. But I was having doubts about the whole business, you know. About God in the first place. An adviser of studies at university suggested coming to the Holy Land.'

'Did you come directly to Israel?'

'No, Lebanon and then Jordan,' I said.

'Did you go and see the cedars of Lebanon?' he asked.

'No, but I got their scent in the evening air.'

'When we were kids in the early days in Palestine, we were taken to visit the cedars. We kids used to link hands and try and reach round the trunks of the biggest trees,' he said. And there was nostalgia in his voice.

'I went to the ruins at Baalbeck. And I went to Sidon, to the Second World War cemetery there.'

'Why the cemetery?'

'Someone back home had been at the Commando raid at the Litani river, and he asked me to visit the cemetery.'

'I was at the Litani river in June '41 at the time of that raid,' Reuben said. 'I was in the Palmach, a Jewish unit from Palestine. We were guides to the Australians who were to cross the river after the commandos knocked out the heavy gun emplacements.' He grinned broadly, 'Later on, I was in the British army when the British formed the Jewish Brigade. I was in the Jewish Brigade.' And he smiled, and went over to the charge-hand of our group.

Spurred by his words about my work, and his being in the Palmach unit at the Litani raid, I spent an afternoon in Tiberias and got my first roll of film developed. And then I sent a couple of prints of the war graves at Sidon to the elder back home.

Earlier, I'd come across what seemed to have been at one time a raised bed, containing cactus, not far from the last of the remaining wooden huts. The members' accommodation was well laid out, and there were broad swathes of grass and quite a

143

few trees. Near the last of the wooden huts ran a connecting earth-beaten track to a metalled path, and close to this intersection, about two yards in from the metalled path was this crumbling raised bed. It was about seven feet long and perhaps thirty inches wide. Its retaining walls were loose rocks, and where the top row still remained was about thirty inches high. Two or three young pine had taken root and were growing about three feet from the western side; their lateral branches formed what was almost a screen that set off the remaining succulents.

I remembered that in Old Testament times, Nehemiah re-built the broken down walls of Jerusalem. I mulled over the idea. All right, a little more modest, but I would try and take on a project on my own, not as part of a team, and have a go at rebuilding the raised bed. *Laborare est orare* (to work is to pray) also came to mind. Perhaps a project like this, on my own, by the Sea of Galilee where Jesus taught, would have the effect of shoring up my crumbling set of beliefs.

I asked Amos about the site.

'Years ago one of the members was an expert on cactus. He taught himself all about them. He built it. After he died no one bothered with it.'

'What if I have a go at rebuilding it?'

'If you want. It's up to you. We didn't get rid of it because some of the flowers are beautiful. We just cut grass round it.'

So I went to the farm steading, told them why I wanted it and they gave me a hessian sack. I emptied my rucksack, put the hessian one inside as an inner lining; and each afternoon, after a few hours sleep, but before going for a swim in Kinneret, I left the kibbutz, crossed the highway and foraged for suitable rocks. I reckoned that I could carry about twenty kilos in weight at a time; and I started ferrying the rocks to the site. After a few days, Amos appeared with one of the jeeps; and we loaded and unloaded rocks together. It helped speed up the process, but he left me to get on with the building of it on my own.

I was delighted with the result. My project was puny in comparison with Nehemiah's, but I had followed on from the labours of another man; it was restorative; and it enhanced nature. But as for bolstering my faith . . . How could I have known then that I would come away from it bearing the mark of Cain?

I didn't mean to kill the man. I intended to stun him so that the guard could disarm him. But now his body was lying on the ground at my feet, the skull smashed. The butt of his pistol was still warm from his grasp when I took hold of it. My knees began to tremble, and I had to brace the back of my thighs against the low retaining wall as I held the weapon. I felt I was going to vomit. Within the space of five minutes, I'd fallen straight into the deepest pit in hell from the sublime sunlit heights.

Her name was Rebecca. She came and sat beside me at an evening meal. She was an American, a New Yorker, with short, dark hair, grey-green eyes and she had attractive skin. She was probably about twenty-five. She'd arrived three days earlier, but I hadn't seen her up until now for she worked in the kitchen. I'd been pointed out to her as another Anglophone. I was suntanned by now, and in my working rig at breakfast or lunch in the dinning hall, I could have passed for a Sabra.

She was happily voluble that first evening. In her spare time, she worked as a volunteer with a Jewish youth group in New York; she had taken a month's leave from her job — she had a degree in commerce and was worked in marketing — to research whether it was feasible to send out a group of high school graduates to work in the kibbutz for a summer.

I was flattered she decided to join me; and after the meal we went to the culture centre and spent an hour and a half, chatting quietly, so as not to distract the two or three readers. Then Rebecca invited me to come to her 'apartment', as she put it, for a fruit juice. She was accommodated in the new generation of concrete buildings. Her living quarters were cooler than the wooden hut. We sat and talked for ages; although, as time went on I had a gnawing worry reminding me every half hour that I had to be awake at 3.30am. What held me back from taking my leave of her was my increasing certainty, the longer we talked, from Rebecca's body language, from the relaxed, confident way she sat back in her chair and the way she looked at me, and held my gaze, that if I made an approach she wouldn't object. It wasn't a difficult choice: the flesh easily got the better of my work-ethic mind-set. We kissed awkwardly — she in the chair, I on my knees beside her. I stood up and so did she. We embraced. I turned us gently to her left, towards her bed. 'Not tonight, Napoleon,' she said.

But three nights later, when I left and clicked the door latch of her room, I paused for a moment, looking around; the delicate night air added to my euphoria. It was almost 1.30am; a working day lay ahead, and I couldn't have cared less.

The grounds were not all that well-lit, but there were modest lamp posts giving out soft light, and the trees cast shadows. It was attractive and quiet at night. There would be no one about at this hour. Rather than double back to a metalled path that ran alongside an avenue of deciduous trees and forked a little way beyond, I cut diagonally across grassed areas from Rebecca's, reached first one of the paths about twenty yards from where it had forked and headed across the grass for the other one. When I got to it, instead of carrying on to the wooden buildings and my hut, I strolled the few yards to the intersection with the earth-trodden track and the site of the restored cactus bed. Proud of my work, I couldn't resist walking past it.

I had come abreast of it, when I registered very faint sounds behind me and to my left. My first response was to feel guilty; I had an irrational urge to conceal myself. This would be the guard on his rounds; if he saw me heading to my hut at this hour, he would put two and two together; kibbutz gossip was like a small town; I would be teased from now on; it would be embarrassing. Almost as a reflex action and without thinking it through, I stepped swiftly to the right and behind the shelter of the young pine that grew beside the raised bed. I was wearing a navy-blue short sleeve shirt and denim shorts; so when he passed along the metalled path, within an arm's length of me, the guard wouldn't see me.

I stood stock-still. Then I saw two figures emerge from the dark screen of the avenue of trees. Suddenly, from some depths within me, a hard-wired, primitive survival instinct came alive and took command. And I simply knew, in a millisecond — they were a threat.

They ran from the dark avenue, bending forward slightly from the waist. Then I saw each carried a weapon. They stopped ten yards from where I stood. One gave a swift hand signal to the second, who ran across the grass towards the further away metalled path. Then the one who signalled ran straight towards my hiding place. I ducked down below the top of the retaining wall, and held my breath, separated from him by thirty inches. I screened out the night insects. At first there was not a sound. Then I heard it — a footfall and another, the soft tread of rubber-soled boots, not the flap of sandals. It was the guard.

I raised my head until my eyes were an inch above the level of the top row of rocks. With the faint glow of lamp standards in the background there was enough ambient light for me to see the man framed between two cacti; he was in combat fatigues; he had his back to me. There was a faint click; he stretched to his left and skewed his body from the waist slightly until I could see the pistol he held.

He was going to kill the guard.

I had to act. If I called out a warning this intruder would turn round and put a bullet into me, with still time to have advantage over the guard.

My right hand felt its way along the top rocks of the wall I'd restored, until my fingers enclosed the narrower end of one that yielded when I flexed my wrist; I lifted a four-kilo rock. There was a slight trickling of the soil I disturbed. But the man was concentrating to his front. I held the rock with both hands. The footfalls came closer; the man in front of me tensed himself; I straightened up, quickly side-stepped clear of the wall, taking all my weight on my left foot and I raised the rock just above my head. But my movement alerted the man, and he swivelled round from the waist holding his weapon. He was almost in profile. Fear gave me savage speed and strength. I lunged forward on to my right foot and my downswing with the rock caught him on the skull.

Spatters of dew from overhanging branches fell on my forehead. The human frame in front of me crumpled to the earth. I cried out. Almost instantly a beam of light flashed over the body and then blinded me. Then the light went back to the man on the ground. In that brief moment I saw the matted black hair, oozing blood and shards of shattered bone. I let the rock fall from my grasp. The guard, recognizing me, switched off the flashlight. He drew his pistol from the holster, and spoke in a hoarse whisper in Hebrew, then changed to English, 'How many?'

'One more. He ran that way,' I said, pointing.

The guard acted decisively; he bent down, picked up the man's pistol, checked it, put it in my hand, and said, 'Wait here. Maybe their rendezvous

149

point.' Then he guided my fingers on the weapon and said, 'Safety off. On. OK?' Without waiting, he left me but didn't follow the route the second man had taken: he moved out of my sight below where I stood, and ran, pistol in hand, across the grass at an angle to intersect the other path.

I felt weak. I was going into a faint. I had killed a fellow man. 'Oh God forgive me. Help me,' I prayed.

Suddenly, two pistol shots in quick succession rang out. Instinct took over, banishing contrition in an instant. I tested the extent the safety catch had to move from on to off. And I waited.

After what seemed an eternity, there were voices. Then I saw the beams of flashlights, and the silhouettes of kibbutzniks fanning out in a line. Two beams of light finally came my way and the guard and another kibbutznik arrived, one on either side of me. A beam stayed on the man on the ground, the other flicked over me and stayed a moment or two on the rock I'd used.

'There were only two you saw?' the other kibbutznik said. He was armed with a short automatic weapon.

'Yes, only two.' The newcomer stretched out his hand and took the dead man's pistol from me.

'Come and look at the other one,' the guard said, 'see if it's the second man you saw. There may be more than two.'

I followed the guard at a quick trot and was aware that someone else with a flashlight had appeared on the scene and joined the kibbutznik with the automatic.

The second raider had been hit by the guard's bullets in the head and the chest. He lay sprawled beside a tree. 'Yes, that's him. From his build, I think that was the other one,' I said. I was aware, though, that the others were not standing about as spectators: there seemed to be a drill they were following. A man would come running up and although I didn't know what he was saying, I could guess he was making a report. They were checking areas like the children's block and reporting back. In the group I felt stronger.

One of those who came up and reported was Amos. After he made his report, he came over to me. 'You OK?'

'Yes,' I managed to get out.

'You did well, I hear.' And that was it. There was nothing more that needed to be said. These men were seasoned veterans of wars and insurgency.

From the south came the unmistakable whirr of a helicopter. Soon we could see its lights and it touched down beyond our sight closer to Kinneret. Within minutes, it rose up in the air again and flew a pattern to the west. Amos told me that it would be patrolling above the highway, looking for a vehicle that might be waiting to extract the two raiders; they would have intended to get rid of their uniforms before daylight. And then the heavily armed soldiers who disembarked from the helicopter went fanning out across the living areas checking them out.

An hour later we were all gathered in the dining hall for what someone said to me was an appraisal of what happened. The military had declared the kibbutz site clear. The soldiers were grouped round a table, and had been supplied with tea and coffee. The kibbutz team and the army officer and I were round a table near the kitchen. It was strange: a serious discussion, gathering facts to make an evaluation, and in a tongue I could not follow. But I knew I would be called upon and I was prepared. The army officer had been listening, rather than contributing; then he spoke to the security team convenor, who turned to me.

'You were the first to see them. Where were you, and where were they?'

I knew I had to be economical with the truth and omit that I thought it was the guard I'd heard, and I was concealing myself from him. But I told them that I'd been with Rebecca and the route I'd taken.

'They came down the screened side of the trees?' the kibbutznik asked.

'Yes, but I was far enough away as I crossed over not to register with them?'

'But from that distance, how did you know they were not two of us?'

'I can't explain it,' I said, 'some instinct told me they were a threat, from the way they moved. I stepped aside and waited until I was sure.'

The appraisal continued in Hebrew, and I wasn't brought back into it until the final summation. The army officer said in English, 'Good you were there. They must have had surveillance of the guard's routes and the paths he took.' Some more discussion followed, but the focus was now on the guard, and I could sense they were discussing changing the patrol patterns. Chair legs scraping along the floor were the signal it was over. But the guard came across to me, and with a warm smile held out his hand to me, and said, 'Thank you.'

I shook his hand, and said, 'I don't know your name.'

'Leon,' he said. As he said it, the army officer and Amos came up and joined us. 'It is best if you don't go to bed now. It's better for you to work today, no matter how tired you are,' the officer said.

'Take a shower. You have blood on you,' Amos said.

Only when I was in the shower area where there were mirrors did I realize the state I was in. It had not been moisture from the trees I felt but the man's lifeblood. My shirt was done for. 'Blood stains won't come out once they've set.' My mother's scolding tones when she saw the mess I was in after that fight at primary school came back to me now. She would never know from me how I came to ruin this navy blue shirt. I really liked it: its collar lay so well, and the neck and the cut of the shoulders were perfect. A few years back I would have worn a shirt like this to the school summer dance. God, I thought, from scrapping in the playground to this; and I couldn't help it: I cried like a child.

The aftermath was something else. I was glad of the army officer's advice, for while the work did not demand mental effort, being with others in the banana groves and sharing the water butt breaks together helped me come out of an endless loop of what if — what if I'd left Rebecca's earlier? What if I'd tried to grapple the weapon from him?

At around eleven, Reuben appeared in his jeep. 'You'll not be needed in the follow-up,' he said.

'What do you mean?'

'Follow-up to an armed incursion is handled by the military. The civil authorities aren't involved. The military have reported to the UN Peace Monitoring Group that there was a breach of the cease-fire, and handed over the bodies. Killed by the guard and an unarmed member of the kibbutz, they've said. This afternoon two UN officers will come here with two of our senior officers.'

I nodded my understanding.

'The idea is for the UN to trace the source: whether it's from Jordan or Syria. They try and call them to account at cross-border meetings.'

The worst time, though, was when I was alone. I wrestled with alternatives. What could I have done differently? And the longer I thought about it, the more I knew the answer — nothing. Thomas Hardy was spot on in *Tess of the D'Urbervilles* when he wrote that this is a blighted planet. Violent death stalked Galilee that night. At least one person was bound to die; and I'd become part of a permutation because I had guiltily tried to conceal myself from the guard. There was no escaping that reality.

But the enormity of what I had done in following primitive instinct that night forced me to pray to God, even although I had come to no longer believe in God.

When I'd left home, there wasn't any room in my rucksack for books, but I'd managed one: the slim paperback *Letters and Papers from Prison* of Dietrich Bonhoeffer. Bonhoeffer was a German Lutheran pastor who was executed by the Nazis; he believed Adolf Hitler should be assassinated; and he was part of the underground group that planned it. In extreme circumstances, he reasoned, you have to act; you have to accept responsibility. And you have to live with the consequences. I read and reread his poignant letter of 21 July 1944, when he knew that the attempt to assassinate Hitler the day before had failed. He understood the price of that failure.

Hoping, perhaps, for some sign, for something positive, some reassurance I could take for myself, one afternoon, I walked along the shore of the lake from the kibbutz the few miles to the ruins of the synagogue at Capernaum where Jesus taught. The Syrian hills rose up from the water with the same profile they had two thousand years ago.

There was no one at the ruins. Evergreen trees, twelve to fifteen feet high, had grown from blown seed around the outer wall. The temple that now lay in ruins had itself been built on top of the synagogue where Jesus spoke, but parts of the original wall remained; and I stood on the basalt floor, by the three-foot high walls of the earlier synagogue, on which carved blocks of the original pillars and some of the friezes had been tidily placed. According to biblical scholars, Mark is the earliest of the gospels; and Mark tells that Jesus taught and astonished his listeners in this synagogue with his teaching. But the gospel doesn't go into the content of what he taught. I put my hand on the wall. The words of Jesus would have echoed from these stones. Now the stones were as silent as the pagan ruins at Baalbek.

It was impossible to get to grips with the teachings of Jesus without the help of biblical scholars. So I thought about the people he recruited as followers, and fishermen came first to mind. What prompted fishermen to follow him?

Fish from Kinneret was a part of our diet, and also an important commodity, especially the delicious St Peter's fish, and provided income for the kibbutz. The method they found effective was night fishing. I watched them set out one night. There were two open boats, ten feet long, with a boom structure on the stern projecting about four feet beyond, on which were fixed powerful lights. The lights attracted the fish from the depths to near the surface and they were netted.

In my experience, men who work with their hands tend to be rational in their judgements, not readily inclined to change sensible work habits or jump into new jobs at the drop of a hat. I found it hard to image kibbutznikim packing in their work and leaving it all if the Messiah came to Galilee. There were no signs, no answers at Capernaum or Kinneret.

I went round to Rebecca's on the evening of Shabbat. I did it openly, but I didn't feel like some hotshot Neanderthal slouching back to the cave and his woman after a hard day's foraging. What had happened was having an effect on my relationship with Rebecca.

And it dawned on me: I'd been hit by a double whammy. I'd been in a fool's paradise thinking I had left my religious moral precepts at the bottom of the Mediterranean: Poseidon spewed them back at me. And I was associating my guilt at killing the insurgent with my guilt for having slept with Rebecca — because, of course, according to my religion's thought police, it was lustful coupling that really got God's goat, not killing a fellow man.

We were sitting side by side on her bed. I brought all that baggage out into the open, and shared it.

'Neil, get rid of that thinking first thing in the morning or your day will be shot to shit,' Rebecca said, taking my hand in hers.

I smiled weakly. She was tough-minded all right, 'Yes, but that's the problem?'

'There's only one way to do it! All we have is our rational mind,' she said. 'A guilt-obsessed religion damages you emotionally. You've got to question those thoughts rationally, ruthlessly.'

I nodded. As we talked, I saw really for the first time what I've come to ascribe to women much more than men: capacity for insight into a partner.

'You took a life to save a life. Perhaps more than one. You could have been on your way from a prayer vigil that night. What you were doing before it happened isn't related to it.'

Talking together in that vein helped. We sat holding hands. Then, after a while, Rebecca said, 'Let's go to bed.'

We lay together. I gained strength from her. We made love, and there was comfort and tenderness in our embrace.

I wakened not long after dawn. Horizontal rays of light projected on to the wall at our heads from the lower blades of the window shutters. Rebecca's hair was tumbling on the pillow close to my face. I lay looking at her, asleep on her side facing me. She was lovely, supportive and trusting; and she was mature. She was tired by the hard physical work in the kibbutz kitchen; she brought out a strong protective streak in me. I didn't go back to sleep; I lay there and marvelled. Lines from the Book of Proverbs came to mind where the writer, in awe, cites examples of nature's imprint that are too wonderful to express in words: the way of an eagle in the air, the way of a serpent on a rock, and the way of a man with a maid.

The following Friday we asked for and got the day off. I'd been told that Safed was a popular place with artists. We took a bus there; then we went on to Kiryat Shmona on the Lebanese border to spend Shabbat in a small hotel. I'd wanted to see the border.

'Someone in the kitchen was saying that whichever Arab state is first to make peace with Israel, Lebanon will be the second,' Rebecca said.

We went out in the early evening and looked down a valley into Lebanon. Amos described this time of day as the most attractive, 'when an Arab likes to sit outside the door of his house in the cool evening, with his head full of thoughts.' It was a tranquil scene with the dark hue of the hills blending into the gathering darkness. There were no guard towers, no gun emplacements: the border between Israel and Lebanon consisted of two strands of a rusting barbed-wire fence. And the purple hills were indifferent to man's hostilities.

Rebecca's time at the kibbutz came to an end. She was taking a bus to Tiberias and then another to Tel Aviv to the airport for an evening flight to New York. I carried her rucksack to the kibbutz road end and we boarded the bus. In Tiberias, Rebecca had an hour to wait before the connecting bus to Tel Aviv, but there was a lot of milling around at the bus station, and quite soon a queue formed. We stood in the queue together, so there wasn't much opportunity for private talk. Perhaps it was as well. She had her career; I had still to start mine. We had formed a bond with all that had happened; one that lasted over time and at a distance. When I next saw Rebecca it was in New York, seven years later, and she was happily married with two children.

I wasn't in a rush to get back to the kibbutz, so long as I got there in time for the evening meal. I went first to look at the Ottoman wall by the lake, and then, mulling over what I knew of its history, I wandered along some of the streets of Tiberias, the city founded in the early years of the Christian Era and named after the Roman Emperor, Tiberius. It had been an important city in the Roman Empire for a time. Then mentally I switched channels and thought about my trip to the Holy Land. It had turned out to be a far cry from spiritual renewal; spiritually, I was all over the place; I was lost.

If, at that moment though, the Oracle at Tiberias had read my mind and spoken and said, 'Hold on. Not so fast. You have known a woman; you have taken a life; but you have not completed the hat trick: when you bring home what is lost, you will find the road to take,' I would probably have thought — typical oracle: cryptic and phoney. And I would have been wrong.

I was driving a tractor on higher ground west of the kibbutz, looking down on the Sea of Galilee when it happened.

Reuben checked that I had a driver's licence, and then assigned me to the task with another man, Danny. On the second morning, however, Danny was transferred to another project at the last moment and so I was working on my own.

We had been clearing new ground on the higher slopes for cultivation. A track had been made, wide enough and more for a tractor; and coarse, long grass had been cut down and left in piles at regular intervals by the side of the track. Long, thistle-like plants were dried out but they were rough to handle.

Down below me to the east, lay Kinnert in the basin formed at the base of the slopes. In the early morning's silver light, a faint mist rose lazily from its surface. To the west, rolling hills and U-shaped valleys gradually took shape.

The tractor was an ancient, cantankerous relic; it stalled frequently, and in crabbit old age it resented you when you used the starting handle: unless you were very alert, you risked spraining your wrist when it kicked into life again. I was heading downhill, loading bundles as I came to them, nursing the old tractor, using the clutch gently, hoping it wouldn't stall. I was going to stop for a break at the spot where the driver of a jeep would have left a generous amount of water for two men and also, at this early hour, breakfast for two men. The system they operated was efficient:

rather than ferry groups of two or three from outlying work to the dining hall, a jeep brought breakfast to the site. The order for breakfast was submitted the night before, so I was anticipating breakfast for two men.

At around 7am, I'd got to the water butt and metal panniers with the food, and inspected the breakfast menu: two shelled eggs per man, fresh green salad, lovely bread of a texture you didn't get back home and two dishes of yoghurt. I would have breakfast in instalments this morning I decided. I'd given my hands a good soaking, and was munching an egg and holding a mug of water in the other hand, leaning against the right rear wheel, lulled by the chugging of the engine, until it gave a rasping cough as though it would die on me. I moved to put down my mug of water and lean in and press the accelerator with my hand, when it growled and settled back into a smoother rhythm.

The eye was drawn to the now blue Kinneret. The rock formation here was mainly igneous, as I'd found when I rebuilt the retaining walls of the bed for succulent plants, but about ten or twelve yards to my right there had been a section of softer conglomerate that, over geological time, had eroded to leave a very steep-sided narrow gully, a gorge, only it didn't carry on up the hill to the summit. Its lip was roughly in line with where I had parked the tractor. It was a deep indentation, progressively gouged out as it became a run for water from the hillside; I estimated it might be about fifteen feet across, maybe twenty or thirty feet deep, but it became shallower as it followed the hill slope down to the flat border land round Kinneret.

I picked up another shelled egg from the metal pannier; only two more to go for my second sitting of breakfast, when I heard a lowing — a long plaintive moo coming from further down the same side of the hill. A black and white cow, an Israeli-Holstein from the dairy herd the kibbutz had, was plodding up the slope on the far side of the gully, an area that might not have been kibbutz land for all I knew. The herd was kept in the byre; this one must have got out somehow and made its way across the highway and up in to higher ground. I focused on the cow and speculated how it could have got this far.

She was making good progress up the slope and was roughly in line with me. The cow would have been familiar with a tractor engine's note, I thought; but she was now traversing towards me in a direct line to the edge of the crevasse. I assumed that the animal would sense the danger of a deep drop, but then I remembered that back home, in school days, a farmer's son told me of a sheep falling into a gully and being trapped. I was on tenterhooks as I watched. I didn't want to shout or gesture, but just let the animal make its way. She stopped about three feet from the edge and turned left and plodded uphill.

Soil crumbled down into the gully parallel with her. But she seemed unable to move away from the edge. My heart was in my mouth. She plodded on unperturbed and rounded the top lip of the gully, and came towards me. In the meantime, huffed by lack of attention, the tractor had stalled again. The heavy-eyed cow stood there lowing, pleading. She was thirsty and needed to be milked. I forced myself to act. I got the water butt, took off the lid of a breakfast pannier, and filled it and put it down. The cow's large pink tongue scooped it up in loud slurps.

At that moment I became aware that Reuben's jeep was coming up the hill and was about fifty yards away. I'd been so absorbed with the cow I hadn't heard the jeep.

He got out, gave the cow not much more than a cursory glance, and in his relaxed style came over to the tractor.

'Marilyn's dead,' he said.

'Marilyn . . .?' I tailed off.

He saw the glazed look in my eyes, 'Marilyn Monroe. She took an overdose.'

'No! That's a shame. She was lovely.'

Reuben grinned at me, and then gestured with his head towards the cow, 'You could be like an Arizona cowboy, and take the stray back to the herd.' He rummaged in the back of his jeep and pulled out a coiled rope. The cow, with dripping dewlaps, was unconcernedly slopping up the water, while Reuben skilfully made a loop round its neck and brought the other end to the tractor. 'We'll unhook the trailer,' he said. I pulled out the holding pin; he kept a grip on the rope end in one hand, and we leaned our joint weight against the trailer to inch it away slightly. Then he tied the end of the rope to the tractor's tow-bar. 'Take it nice and slow; she needs to be milked. Must have got out before first light this morning.'

'Did they send out someone on foot to look for the cow?' I asked Reuben.

'No,' and he shook his head, 'Uri's in charge of the herd. He'll wait until they clear up after the milking and then come out looking.' And Reuben grinned broadly, 'Tell him you had to take on a gang of rustlers to get her back. Tell him he needs to be more careful,' and he chuckled.

Even though my mind was elsewhere, on a train of thought with his news that Marilyn had died, I knew I wouldn't be daft enough to follow through on that suggestion.

Then Reuben looked at the trailer, and the pile of vegetation I'd gathered. 'You OK on your own for the rest of the day?' he asked.

'Yes, I'm fine.'

'Take it easy with your steer, pardner,' he said, still chuckling, and got into the jeep, reversed over rough ground, swung back on to the track and drove downhill.

I secured the metal panniers, and turned the old tractor's starting handle until the engine kicked into life, sprang up into the seat as fast as I could before it stalled on me; and I drove slowly down that track.

But I was still thinking about Marilyn. Reuben's words had the sort of effect on me that the Scottish poet Edwin Morgan expressed in his poem 'The Death of Marilyn Monroe':

                     Others die
and yet by this death we are a little shaken, we feel it,
America.

What was Marilyn to me or I to Marilyn that I should feel moved by her death? She had been an ideal, completely unattainable. Yet her luminous presence on screen drew you to her; it was as though you had some relationship with her. The camera lens loved her. But she was vulnerable; and she wanted to be taken seriously as an actress.

I thought about her final movie, *The Misfits*, written for her by her husband, the playwright Arthur Miller. Marilyn's character raged against the roping of the wild mustang ponies. They were to be sold and slaughtered and turned into canned dog food. In one scene, the Clark Gable character, the over-the-hill cowboy, roped the wild mustang stallion to prove something to himself. But then he released it and the mares and the foal; he set them free for Marilyn's sake.

As the tractor growled its way down the track, Marilyn's death cut through my angst like a keen-edged blade; and I saw it all in a cross section.

I had come on this quest because of my doubts; I'd come searching — as though God was an object I could find evidence of in the Holy Land. Then, for a while, I'd thought that if I found myself I wouldn't need God. The armed incursion put paid to that. I saw now though that searching's a waste of time. Bonhoeffer wrote in one of his letters from prison a thought that gleamed for me: roughly that the only way to be honest is to see that we must live in the world even if there were no God. I resolved, there and then in the tractor's swaying bucket seat, that I would abandon religion; I would revere the wisdom and beauty of the Bible as literature; my lodestone would be my moral intuition; I would do what I believed to be the right thing in life; and I would hold myself accountable.

I saw it simply like that. It was clear to me: I wasn't a lost soul at all. Spiritually, I was strong, stronger than I had been before I set out on this quest.

But some Arizona cowboy on a tractor! There was I with this lost dairy cow that had come to me, mutely insisting on an ancient mutual dependency of man and beast. I kept looking back at her and how she was doing. From my perspective, the cow, broad in the beam, was a small battleship following line astern. Her slender legs, from where I sat, seemed ill-designed for her bulk, but she kept stepping daintily along the track, as I held the old tractor at a gentle walking pace. Then, as we got nearer to the point where I would have to cross the highway, I noticed that my tow rope was hanging more loosely: the cow had the smell of home in her nostrils and had quickened her pace. I felt a sense of delight.

Finding the lost sheep and bringing it back to the fold is a strong metaphor in the New Testament. Well, I was bringing home a lost cow. And I felt elated. The flowing cadence of a verse of Psalm 126 came to me:

> He that goes forth weeping,
> bearing the seed for sowing,
> shall come home with shouts of joy,
> bringing his sheaves with him.

It became the source for a hymn that wasn't really part of my Presbyterian tradition. But before we reached the road leading down to the kibbutz, the air reverberated as I sang lustily in my best tenor voice the only lines I knew of it:

> Bringing in the sheaves, bringing in the sheaves,
> We shall go rejoicing, bringing in the sheaves,

while the thrawn tractor's grating engine notes supplied the bass.

A few evenings before I left the kibbutz, there was a get-together in the open air. It was a beautiful night. I'd never seen so many stars; and there was a silver sickle of moon high above Kinneret. These get-togethers were a custom they had from time to time. Everyone seemed to be there, young and old. Amos produced a bottle of wine and poured some into a plastic cup. 'L'*chaim*' (to life), he said, and we raised the toast to life.

'It's really good,' I said.

'It's made in the traditional style of winemaking in Palestine'. If that was true, at the last supper, Jesus and his disciples weren't drinking anything as revolting as church communion wine.

The flames flickered, the faces shone in the firelight. There is something primitive about campfires that makes people want to sing in accord. Some of the songs had a strong nostalgic flavour of Russian folk music. But I was not allowed to be a spectator when it came to singing and dancing the *Hava Nagila*, which means let us rejoice; and I joined hands and linked into the big circle.

I wrote to my adviser in studies at the university, telling him that the trip to the Holy

Land had resolved my doubts; I would not be matriculating for divinity, but I hoped to call in on him during my first leave. At home, before I left to join my intake at the military academy, I had an appointment with the elder who had paved the way for the journey. As he rose from his desk with his hand outstretched to greet me, I had a flash of insight.

'Were you ever at a cross-roads in your life between a religious vocation and an alternative?'

He looked at me keenly, nodded, and smiled, 'A year of war and reading Kierkegaard was what it took in my case.' And he didn't elaborate.

I adopted that kind of reticence in my twenty-year career defending the realm, which ended with the Falklands Campaign, when, like Fortinbras of Norway, we went to war over an eggshell. Throughout it all I never spoke about my journey to the Holy Land, my time in Israel by the shores of Galilee. I never told my wife; I never told my children; I rarely revisited it in memory: though I'd put my hand to the sword and not to the plough and only on the Bible in an oath of allegiance to the Queen, there was no point in looking back.

But now that the tide is running on to that unknown shore, memories drifted along with me tonight when I saw her ghost on television in her last film, *The Misfits*, as I lay propped up by pillows in the hospice bed, on this fiftieth anniversary of Marilyn's death.

Acknowledgements

Several people helped with ideas, information or sources. My thanks go to: Linda Riddell; Rachael Shepherd, Highland Archive Centre; Derek Louden, Tain Museum; John Gordon; Colm Smyth, Professor Sir Tom Devine, University of Edinburgh; Professor Ewen Cameron, University of Edinburgh; Ewan Ross; Gordon Liddell; the Rev George Shand, St Andrew's Scots Memorial Church Jerusalem, David Blake, Curator, Museum of Army Chaplaincy and Colin Campbell, former Member of the Scottish Parliament.

I want to make special mention of Morag Ross Bremner, Manager of Tain Museum, for her support over time with documents and images.

I would like to thank Elizabeth Ross for her advice, Beth Bauman for her critical insights and Anastasia Kemp for her design skills.

Hamish Ross

After National Service in the RAF, he worked in the Scottish education system, in both schools and university and as a senior official in educational administration. His non-fiction books are: *Paddy Mayne*, the acclaimed biography of the revered leader of the wartime SAS, *Freedom in the Air*, the inspiring story of a Czech airman and the dog that flew with him in Bomber Command and *From SAS to Blood Diamond Wars*, with the legendary Fred Marafono; his other fiction work: *Wrongs Hushed Up*, a collection short stories arising out of war and conflict. He was awarded the Commemorative Medal by the Czech Republic for *Freedom in the Air*.